DECKED

THE INVINCIBLES

BOOK ONE

HEATHER SLADE

DECKED
© 2019 Heather Slade

Paperback:
978-1-942200-71-0

decked

/dekt/

past simple and past participle of deck

verb

knocked down; floored; flattened

MORE FROM HEATHER SLADE

TABLE OF CONTENTS

1

Decker

As I drove home from the airport after my flight back from London, something on the side of the road caught my eye. What the hell was that? Couldn't be a deer, not in these parts. It wasn't big enough to be a cow, unless it was a damn skinny one.

I stopped the truck and climbed out, at first thinking it might be a mannequin someone had tossed by the road, until it started to moan.

"*What in the—*" I rushed over and saw it was a woman. It was dark, and she was on her side, but I didn't recognize her. She was pretty enough that if she was from around here, I sure as hell would've.

"Don't move," I said when the woman tried to sit up. I leaned down farther and eased my hand under her head. "Can you tell me what happened?"

"I have to go," she cried, trying again to move. "He'll kill me."

"Who's gonna kill you?"

"My…"

The woman lost consciousness again. But wait, she'd gone perfectly still.

"Lord in heaven," I whispered out loud as I felt for a pulse at the same time I leaned down to check for signs of breathing. Neither were present. I pulled out my phone, called nine-one-one, and then lifted the woman's head slightly to open her airway.

"Nine-one-one operator. What's your emergency?"

"Violet, this is Decker Ashford. I'm just east of mile marker sixty-six on Old Austin Highway. Got a vic, no pulse, not breathing. Starting CPR and rescue breaths. Get somebody out here!"

"On it, Deck. Put me on speaker."

I tossed my phone aside, counted thirty compressions, pinched the woman's nose, and then gave her two rescue breaths before repeating the process.

"Mac says he's two minutes out," I heard Violet say.

Mac? What the hell? Why was she sending the sheriff when the woman wasn't breathing?

I couldn't stop to ask; I'd just finished thirty chest pumps and needed to give her two more rescue breaths. Before I finished the next count, the sheriff's car pulled up, immediately followed by an ambulance.

When the paramedic knelt down next to me, I moved out of the man's way.

As I walked away, something else caught my eye—a cell phone lay not far from the woman.

"What happened here?" Mac asked seconds before two other patrol cars pulled up.

I told him about seeing something alongside the road and how I'd stopped.

"You recognize her?" Mac asked.

"Negative."

"Check for ID?"

"No time, but there's a phone," I answered, pointing to it.

"Can I get some light and a stretcher over here?" I heard the paramedic yell at the same time Mac told one of the deputies to get the phone and put it in an evidence bag.

I saw the blood as soon as the EMTs lifted the woman to put her on the stretcher. The grass below her body was covered in it.

"Gunshot wound is my guess," Mac muttered.

If Mac was right, I had accelerated the woman's death. *"Jesus Christ, I was doing chest compressions."*

Mac put his hand on my shoulder. "You did what you thought needed to be done. Based on what I see, you couldn't have saved her anyway."

I scrubbed my face with my hand. Didn't matter what Mac said, what I'd done was stupid.

"You headed back to the ranch?" Mac asked as we watched the ambulance pull away.

"Nah. I'll follow 'em."

Mac scrunched his eyes. "Decker...this ain't in your jurisdiction."

I shook my head. "I don't have a jurisdiction, Sheriff."

Mac looked over to where his deputies were surveying the scene. "Let's be on our way. Find out the official time of death, and see if we can figure out who this girl was." Before I walked back to my truck, Mac opened the door of the patrol car and grabbed the bag containing the cell and another pair of gloves. "See if you can crack this thing open."

2

Mila

There was an elevator in my building, but I always took the stairs. I liked the exercise, although four flights didn't exactly get my heart rate up.

Tonight, like every other night, I couldn't wait to cross the threshold from the hallway into my studio apartment where I could leave the chaos of the city behind and enter my very own Greek Island oasis.

My walls were painted an aqua blue, and I'd covered my sofa and bed with brightly colored patterns and prints. There were red geraniums in my kitchen, and on my tiny patio, two pots of bougainvilleas. They died every winter, but in the spring, I just planted more.

I tossed my satchel on the end of the bed, kicked off my shoes, removed my hot pink, raw silk blouse, tossed it on the bed too, and then padded into a kitchen that wasn't big enough to fit two people at a time. I opened the refrigerator and pulled out a bottle of rosé.

It was a hot and humid eighty-four degrees outside, even at six in the evening, but inside my apartment, it was a cool seventy-two. One benefit of living in a four-hundred-square-foot space was it didn't take much to cool it in the summer or heat it in the winter. And even as hot as it was, it still was nowhere near the blazing temps of Texas in July.

I unzipped my skirt and tossed it on the pile at the end of my bed, tempted to sit in front of the air conditioner in nothing but my bra and panties. But I couldn't do that. Any minute, my friend and neighbor, Adler, would knock on my door mere seconds before he used the key he kept for emergencies to let himself in.

I had enough trouble trying to convince Ad that I wouldn't date him now or ever—no matter how many times he asked. If he walked in on me scantily attired, he'd assume he'd worn me down enough to change my mind.

It wasn't that I didn't enjoy Adler's company, and he was certainly attractive enough, with his sandy blond hair and hazel eyes. He loved to go to the theater and galleries and roam the streets of Boston, just like I did. He was well-read and a great conversationalist, but when it came to chemistry, there wasn't any. He might as well be my brother, not that I had one.

Then again, maybe it wasn't Adler at all—I was the one with the problem.

I heard Adler's anticipated knock and ducked into the bathroom with my shorts and top in hand.

"Hey," I said, coming out while still fastening the bottom button on my blouse.

"No need to get dressed on my behalf," he said, eyeing the pile of clothes at the end of my bed and then looking me up and down.

"How are you, Ad?"

"Hot," he said, plopping down in the chair I'd been sitting in.

"Glass of wine?" I asked, escaping into the kitchen.

"Sure."

When he leaned back and closed his eyes, I checked him out like he had me.

His signature summer tank looked like he'd had it since he was a teenager. His shorts—too short in my opinion, but it was the style these days—showed off his sculpted legs. Yeah, Ad had a great body. Why didn't it do anything for me? If only it would, I'd know there was hope for me to have a normal life after all.

"I envy how cool your apartment stays."

As far as apartments went, he didn't have much to envy. His was ten times the size of mine. The owners of the building, Adler's parents, had combined all the apartments on the top level into one—and that's where Adler lived. Which meant Adler Livingston was also my landlord.

"How was work today?" he asked, taking the glass of wine I offered.

"Quiet but also productive."

"When are the students back?"

"Officially, not until the end of August. But there are so many workshops going on now."

I worked at my alma mater, the Northeastern College of Music, as an adjunct instructor. It was a step below an adjunct professor, and several steps lower than a tenured professor.

It was my fifth summer as an instructor, and this fall would be the start of my fourth academic year. The private institution, which charged a tuition on par with Harvard but without the same billion-dollar endowment, didn't pay much, but it was enough that I could afford my apartment and occasionally travel.

This year, though, I'd gone through my entire savings, flying back and forth from Texas.

First, it was to visit my ailing grandfather, the man who had taken my sister, our mother, and me in after my parents' divorce, and whom my sister had continued to live with after our mother died shortly after I graduated from high school.

It wasn't just traveling that had left me broke. When my grandfather died, I'd paid the medical bills that the money he left hadn't covered. I'd also paid for the funeral and burial.

My sister, Sybil, had insisted we ask our father to help, but I'd lied and told her the money wasn't an issue. I didn't care if I drained my bank account; I'd never go to that man for money or anything else ever again.

"Oh, by the way, I picked up your mail." Adler pointed to the table near the front door where he'd set it.

"You did? Um...thanks." It was one thing that he had a key to my apartment. I didn't remember anything in my lease that said the landlord kept a key to my mail slot too.

I took another sip of wine and then set it on the table while I flipped through the pile of junk mail. The last piece I came to was from the college.

I picked up my wine and walked over to sit on the end of my bed since Adler was occupying the only chair. I set the glass on the floor and tore open the envelope.

As I skimmed the letter inside, only a handful of words jumped out at me.

> *We regret to inform you that we will not be renewing your contract for the upcoming fall semester.*

"What is it, Millie? You look like you've seen a ghost."

I hated it when he called me Millie. My name was Mila. How fucking hard was that to say? It was the same number of syllables. I folded the paper and shoved it back into the envelope and then went into the kitchen to pour myself more wine. When I came back out, Adler had the letter in his hands.

"Shit, Mila. I'm sorry. They aren't bringing you back?"

I snatched it from his hands and tucked it under a book on my bedside table. "Guess not."

When Adler stood and tried to draw me into a hug, I bristled and backed away. I knew it hurt his feelings, but I couldn't help it. I shook my head to chase away the nightmarish memories of what made me so sensitive to a man's touch. I was already in a horrible mood; I didn't need to add thinking about that to the mix.

"Sorry," he murmured.

"No, I'm the one who's sorry. I'm not going to be very good company, Ad. Why don't you go do something fun with your friends tonight?"

"Because I'd rather hang with you."

"I don't know why," I mumbled, vacillating between being royally pissed off and wanting to cry.

"Because I like you better than anyone else. And someday, you'll like me better than anyone else too," he said, winking at me.

I smiled. It didn't matter that I was behaving like a raving bitch, Adler found a way to disarm me.

He took another drink of his wine. "Come on, let me take you out for dinner at least. It's too damn hot to cook."

He wasn't just sweet, he was always so generous with me. Yeah, he let himself into my apartment, but how many times a week did we go out and he refused to let me pay? At the very minimum, I should accept his invitation graciously. Besides, if I stayed here, all I'd do was wallow in self-pity.

"Okay, but nowhere fancy."

Adler motioned to his shirt and shorts. "Not exactly dressed for black tie, Mil."

"This place is such a tourist trap," I said when he turned right at the corner of Boylston and Dalton.

"You have to admit, their lobstah is wicked pissa."

"Ad, it's too expensive."

"I got you."

I rolled my eyes. "I still have a paycheck coming; I can buy my own dinner." Of course, the only thing I'd be able to afford here was a cup of clam chowder.

"I invited you, remember? My treat."

"Thank you," I murmured.

"Wine?" he asked when we were seated at the crowded bar.

"I'd rather have a beer."

Adler raised an eyebrow.

"It's just so hot."

"You don't need to convince me. Two Mystics when you get a chance," he said to the bartender before turning back to me.

"Let's talk about something besides the job. I'm sure you'll get another one lined up in no time. How's your sister doing? Have you spoken to her recently?"

How's my sister? What an odd thing for Adler to ask. He'd only met Sybil once, and I'd always been forthright about our lack of a relationship. Not to mention, bringing up Sybil reminded me of the state of my now-empty savings account and the fact that I no longer had a job in order to replenish it.

"I'm sure she's fine," I answered, wondering if she really was. The last time I was in Texas, we'd argued to the point where I changed my ticket and returned to Boston ahead of schedule. Since, I'd had an inexplicable feeling that something was up with Sybil. Not that I'd call to find out. My sister and I had never gotten along, even when we were children.

I took a long swig from the bottle of beer the bartender set in front of me.

"You okay?" Adler asked, resting his hand on my arm.

I bristled at his touch like I had earlier. "Yeah, I'm just tired."

He frowned. "Why do you do that?"

"I'm sorry. I just..."

"Don't like being touched. Yeah, I get it." He got off the stool and went in the direction of the men's room.

When he came back, he acted as though nothing uncomfortable had happened. I did my best to pay attention as he rambled on about his day, but I couldn't stop my mind from drifting back to losing my job and why I suddenly had a bad feeling about my sister.

After dinner, I let Adler talk me into going to a concert at a park a few blocks from our building. We sat in the grass, and I closed my eyes, letting the smooth jazz wash away my worries—at least temporarily.

I must've dozed off, but I woke with a start when I felt Adler touch my arm.

"Sorry. Your phone was ringing." He handed it to me. "I think it was your sister."

I groaned, remembering the weird feeling I'd had earlier.

"Be right back," I said, standing and walking over to the sidewalk where I'd be better able to hear when my sister answered. The voice I heard, though, was a man's.

"Hello, this is Sheriff MacIver calling from Hays County in Texas. You are listed in a woman's phone as the emergency contact."

I felt my stomach drop. "That would be my sister, Sybil Knight. Has something happened?"

"Ma'am, is there somewhere you can take a seat?"

"Why?"

The man cleared his throat. "A woman we believe might be your sister was found outside of Austin, Texas, this evening. I'm sorry, Miss Knight, but…"

"*But, what?*" I shrieked. I saw Adler stand and walk in my direction. Several other people were staring at me.

"We haven't been able to confirm her identity, but if it is your sister—again, I'm sorry, ma'am—but she's dead."

3

Decker

It had taken exactly three seconds for me to get into the dead woman's phone. Didn't people know by now that the first password someone would try was *password*?

I looked up when Mac walked out of his office.

"What did you find out?"

Mac motioned for me to come in and closed the door.

"Reached the sister. Her name is Mila Knight. If it's her, our victim is Sybil Knight."

"Knight? The name sounds familiar."

"You're probably thinking of Judd Knight, their father."

"Whatever happened to him?"

Mac shook his head. "He and their mother—I think her name was Nancy—divorced damn near twenty years ago. I haven't seen any of them around these parts since the girls were little. I remember hearing that Nancy died. Can't remember when that was exactly, at least ten years, though."

"If the mother is dead, wouldn't Judd be next of kin?"

"The sister's already on her way to identify the body."

Poor woman. First, she lost her mother, and now, her sister. "Where's she flying in from?" I asked.

"Boston, of all Godforsaken places." John "Mac" MacIver believed anywhere outside of the great State of Texas was Godforsaken. The sheriff scrubbed his face with his hand. "It's always hard to tell someone their loved one is dead, but over the phone…"

I'd never had to do it; I didn't envy Mac's position.

"After I broke the news, someone else came on the line. A man. He was the person who confirmed she'd come and identify the body."

"When's she flying in?"

"Tomorrow."

"I'll see you then."

"This isn't your responsibility, Decker. Go home and get some rest."

"I found her. The sister will have questions."

"I'll send her your way if she does."

I waited until I got back to the ranch, where I lived and worked, to pull my second cell out of the truck's console. I stuck it in my pocket, grabbed the takeout food I'd picked up when I left the airport hours ago, and went inside.

I set the two phones and my food on the kitchen counter and went into my office to power up the monitors. There hadn't been a whole lot going on here in the last week, and it would be fine with me if it stayed that way.

Summer was typically a slow season, but this year, more would fall on my shoulders than usual. Quint Alexander, the ranch's owner, was away for a month on the honeymoon he and his wife had been trying to plan since January. Not that I minded the extra responsibility. I'd lived and worked on this ranch since I was thirteen years old, and had been the ranch manager since I was twenty-three, when Quint and I took over running it full-time.

Before that, Quint's father—who everyone called Z—had run it, usually with Quint and me by his side. When he felt we were ready, Z announced his retirement from ranch life and returned to London where he was currently Chief of Her Majesty's Secret Intelligence Service, otherwise known as MI6.

I never met Z's late wife and Quint's mother. She'd died before I came to live on the ranch. She was the one who inherited the property from her daddy, Wasp King.

Hell, even before I knew a thing about the Alexanders, I'd heard stories about ol' Wasp. Just about everyone in this part of Texas had. If I remembered correctly, Wasp and Judd Knight, father of the dead woman, had been tight at one time, even though Judd was several years Wasp's junior.

Walking back into the kitchen, I opened the take-out container of Mexican food, dumped half of it into a bowl, and stuck it in the microwave. It was close to one in the morning, and the last thing I should be doing was eating food likely to give me heartburn, but I hadn't eaten since before I left the UK.

I'd been there for a friend's wedding, and on the day before I left, I'd been invited to attend an impromptu meeting for a start-up business. It was the kind of side work I already did in addition to my work at the ranch, only instead of being contracted when needed, I'd be a founding partner of the new company.

It was tentatively named Invincible Intelligence and Security Group—a name as long as it was pretentious—not that I gave much of a shit about stuff like that.

The meeting had been called by Cortez "Rile" DeLéon. Rile's father, Carlos DeLéon, Duke of Soria, was the youngest brother of King Felipe VI of Spain. Rile's mother was eighth cousin to Elizabeth II, Queen of the United Kingdom. With dual citizenship and connectivity to royalty, Rile had become an early asset to MI6.

The other two men at the meeting were Keon "Edge" Edgemon and Miles "Grinder" Stone. Both men were with MI5—the national intelligence side of England's secret service.

All three men were ready to leave formal employment and strike out on their own. I, on the other hand, had always been a private contractor. The idea that I'd have more administrative responsibilities with this new entity didn't thrill me, and I'd said so.

Rile had asked me to stay behind when the meeting adjourned. "We need you, Decker," he'd said. "Please consider joining us."

The man hadn't insulted me with sanctimonious platitudes, and that was the only reason I even considered accepting the offer. I knew exactly how good I was, and I didn't need anyone blowing smoke up my ass to confirm it.

Before I walked out, I promised Rile an answer within the week. First, I needed to talk the proposal over with the two men who had been my mentors for most of my life—Z Alexander and Laird "Burns" Butler.

Z was well aware of the new venture but told me to think it over before we spoke.

It was likely Burns was equally aware. Nothing in the intelligence world escaped the man who was renowned worldwide for his contributions to security technology—my specialty. I was good, but Burns was the best in all the world.

I walked back into the kitchen, dumped the food sitting in the microwave into the trash, and went to bed. It had been a long damn day, and something told me tomorrow wouldn't be much better.

4

Mila

"I'm coming with you. This isn't something you should do on your own," Adler said as we stood at the airline ticket counter the next morning.

"This isn't your responsibility. I can pay for my own airfare."

When I pulled out my wallet, Adler covered my hand with his. "Please, let me do this," he said.

I nodded, trying my hardest not to jerk my hand away. I was too exhausted and overwrought to argue with him.

Last night, after I'd dropped my phone with the news of my sister's death, Ad had picked it up and finished the conversation with the man I'd been talking to.

"They've asked you to come and identify the body," he'd said after the car service he'd called dropped us off at our building and he walked me to my apartment.

"Of course," I'd murmured. "When?"

"Tomorrow morning."

Adler had stayed with me, saying he'd sleep better if he knew I was okay, even if it meant sleeping in the chair.

I followed him through the security line and up to the waiting TSA agent. I handed him my boarding pass and ID.

"Sure is hot in Texas this time of year," the man said, attempting polite conversation.

"Yes," I responded when he handed back my documents, wishing people would stop trying to make small talk with me.

"You have a nice day, miss," I heard him say as I stepped aside to wait for Adler. A nice day? It would be the worst day of my life—identifying the body of my sister, my last surviving family member—since I no longer considered my father as family.

When we exited security at the Austin-Bergstrom International Airport, Adler excused himself to the men's room. I was waiting a short distance down the concourse when I saw a man holding a sign with my name on it.

"I'm Mila Knight," I said, approaching him.

The man lowered the sign, held out his hand, and I shook it. "Decker Ashford."

I knew the name. Could it be the same Decker Ashford? It had to be. It wasn't exactly a common name. Not to mention I'd never forget the kindness of his striking green eyes or the hint of a smile that he rarely showed, even all those years ago. The only thing that was different, besides his age, was that he no longer had hair that hung past his shoulders. Now, it looked like he kept his head shaved completely bald.

"Did Adler arrange for you to pick us up?"

His brow furrowed. "Adler?"

"What about me?" my friend asked, stepping up to my side.

"I thought you'd arranged for a ride."

His eyebrows scrunched as he studied the man who had lowered the sign that bore my name. "I reserved a rental car."

"Um, this is Adler Livingston."

"Decker Ashford," he repeated, not extending his hand to shake Adler's. "I can take you to the medical examiner's office."

"Thank you. That's very nice of you," I murmured, wishing Adler didn't look so irritated. What the hell was his problem? Did he really have to get mad about another person simply being kind?

"Did you check a bag?" Decker asked.

"I just have this carry-on." He took the handle from me and wheeled my bag behind him.

I raised a brow, looked at Adler, and shrugged. Decker hadn't bothered to ask if *he* had checked a bag.

23

"I'm here," Decker said, pointing to an oversized pickup truck. After opening the door and holding out his hand to help me into the front seat, he put the suitcase in the backseat of the cab and left the door open for Adler to climb in behind it with his bag.

At six feet two, poor Ad looked scrunched in the small space. "I can sit back there," I offered.

Before I could open the door to get out, Decker had started the engine and put the truck in gear.

"I'm very sorry for your loss," he said as he pulled out of the parking space.

"Thank you." My eyes filled, and I looked away even though he hadn't turned his head in my direction when he spoke.

"I'm the one who found your sister," he added, leaning toward me as though he didn't want Adler to hear him. "If you have any questions, you can ask."

"Okay. Thank you," I mumbled, brushing away a tear. Questions? I had countless, but I didn't want the answers to any of them.

None of us spoke again until we reached the county building where the sheriff's office and the morgue were located.

"Would you like me to go in with you?" Decker asked as he helped me out of the cab.

I looked at Adler, who appeared not to have heard. He also appeared to still be irritated when he pulled his wallet out.

"What do I owe you?"

I rolled my eyes. Adler could be such a condescending prick sometimes.

"Not a thing," Decker answered, motioning us toward the building's entrance.

I took a deep breath, wishing I could be anywhere but here.

Once inside, Adler stepped up to the desk to let the receptionist know that we had arrived.

"Why did you ask if I wanted you to go in with me?" I asked the man still standing by my side.

"Can't be an easy thing to do."

"Have you ever had to do it?"

He shook his head.

"Your family…" I stopped myself. How many people had deaths in their family that required a body to be identified?

"I don't have any family, ma'am."

Neither did I anymore.

"I'm Sheriff MacIver," another man said, coming out of a door and into the lobby. "Hello, Decker."

"Mac," he responded with a head nod before motioning me to follow the sheriff. He followed too, leaving Adler trailing behind us. Every so often, his fingertips would brush the small of my back. It dawned on me then that every time Decker had touched me, I hadn't flinched.

"Right this way, ma'am," the sheriff said, leading me through another door and down a hallway. I stopped when I saw the sign for the morgue.

"I'll go in with her," I heard Decker say as he grasped the handle and led me into the cold room. I turned to look for Adler, who the sheriff seemed to have engaged in conversation.

"Decker," said an older man who I guessed was the medical examiner.

"This is Mila Knight."

"I'm very sorry to ask you to do this, ma'am."

Not knowing what to say, I followed him over to the table where a body lay covered by a sheet.

"Would you like some privacy?" the medical examiner asked.

I turned and looked into Decker's eyes.

"I'll stay," he said, and I nodded.

He moved the sheet and stepped back.

My sister's lifeless form lay eerily still. "It's her," I whispered, closing my eyes. When I opened them, I was grateful the sheet had been placed back over Sybil's face. "How did she die?" I caught the look that passed between the man and Decker.

"I should have the preliminary results of the autopsy within twenty-four hours. Full results may take up to six weeks to prepare."

"What now?" I asked.

"There's nothing else to be done here," the older man said.

"Is there somewhere else you'd like to go?" Decker asked.

"My sister lived in my grandfather's house in Bluebell Creek. Maybe I should head up there and see about making arrangements."

"If that's where you want to go, I can take you."

"Thank you for your offer. I'm sure Adler won't mind renting a car. He was in Bluebell Creek earlier this year when my grandfather passed away."

"I'm sorry for your loss," Decker muttered as we walked down the hallway to where the sheriff was waiting for us.

"Miss Knight confirmed her sister's identity," Decker said before the sheriff asked or I could speak for myself.

The sheriff nodded and turned to me. "I have your contact information. Here's my card. If you have any questions, don't hesitate to call me."

Too dazed to do anything else, I took the card and tucked it into my small cross-body bag and looked beyond him. "Um, do you know where Adler went?"

The sheriff shrugged. "Last time I saw him, he was outside on his cell phone."

"Okay. Thank you." It seemed odd that he'd leave while I was identifying my dead sister, but I had left him standing in the hallway.

"Will you be staying in town or heading right back to Boston?"

"I'm not sure. I'm thinking of going up to Bluebell Creek."

"It's where her sister lived," Decker added.

"Before you head out, could I have a minute on another subject?" the sheriff said directly to Decker.

"Go ahead," I said when Decker turned to me. "I'll be out front with Ad."

I went outside, but didn't see Adler. A few seconds later, he walked out from the other side of the building.

"Where were you?" I asked.

"Making a call."

Why was he being so short with me? It was so unlike him.

"If you need to get back…"

"What about you? Is there any reason you need to stay here?"

I stared at him. Was he serious? I folded my arms.

"What?" He reached out to touch my arm, but pulled back.

"You didn't even ask me about Sybil."

"Right. Um. Sorry. Distracted. It was an important call. Are you doing okay?"

"Am I doing okay? *Adler!* I just walked into a morgue and saw my dead sister lying on a metal table under a sheet. *No! I'm not doing okay!*" I dissolved into tears, and when he tried to comfort me, I pulled away.

"I'm sorry, Mil. I don't know what else to say."

I looked at him and shook my head, but before I could say anything more, Decker came out of the building.

"There's been a change of plans." He walked over and put his hand on my shoulder. "Mila, I'm sorry to have to tell you this, but the house in Bluebell Creek is a crime scene. There won't be any access to it until the sheriff gives his okay."

Adler made no secret of the fact he noticed that I didn't flinch or pull away when Decker touched me. I couldn't explain my reaction—or lack of reaction— myself. Decker Ashford, a man I barely knew, made me feel safe. Was it just his kindness? Was it that he took charge in a way that didn't threaten me but, instead, made me feel protected? Or was it because all those years ago, he'd done the same thing?

"The sheriff asked me to bring this to you." Decker held up a bag.

"What is it?"

"Your sister's effects."

I looked into his eyes. "I don't know what to do," I whispered.

"Take your sister's stuff, and we'll go back to Boston. When the sheriff says it's okay, we can come back."

I looked over at Adler and then back at Decker. "How long do you think it will be?"

"It's difficult to say."

When I turned back to Ad, he was studying something on his phone. Why was he on his phone? "There's a flight in two hours," he mumbled. "If you hurry, we can catch it."

Decker took a step closer. "If you need a place to stay, there's a guest house at the ranch."

"The ranch?"

"King-Alexander. It isn't too far from here."

Adler was still preoccupied by his phone. Here was a man I hadn't seen since I was a child—and barely knew then—being kinder to me than the man who had been one of my closest friends for the last four years.

"If you're sure," I said to Decker, again appreciating how sensitive he was being.

"I'm sure."

"Give me a minute?"

He nodded and stepped away.

"I'm staying here. At least until they can determine my sister's cause of death."

Adler finally looked up from his phone. "I don't see the point, Mil. Whether you're here or at home, isn't going to change anything. Let's get back to Boston, and when there's something more you're needed for here, you can come back."

"Something more I'm needed for? Adler—" God, I couldn't even talk to him. *Needed for?* My sister was dead. I had a funeral to plan, a burial, and then I had to figure out what to do with my grandfather's house. Wasn't any of this dawning on him? "I'm going to stay, but you should go home."

His eyes opened wide as though something I'd said surprised him. Again, I was stunned by his insensitivity. Had he always been this way and I just never noticed? Or had I noticed and just overlooked it because it had always been easier just to accept that Adler was always around, always doing things for me?

"I'm not leaving without you."

"I'm sure you'd be welcome to stay at the ranch."

Adler grabbed my arm. "No, Mila, I'm not staying at the ranch or anywhere else. I'm getting on the next plane to Boston, and so are you."

"Let her go." Decker stalked over to us and got in Adler's face until he dropped my arm. I hadn't noticed before how much taller than Adler he was. He had to be at least six feet five, maybe more.

"This is our ride," Adler said when a car pulled up. He'd called a car service? Was that what he'd been doing? "Are you coming with me or not?"

"I've told you more than once that I'm staying here."

Adler looked at me and then at Decker, who stood next to me with his arms folded.

"Last chance," said the man I'd believed to be my friend. When I shook my head, he climbed into the back seat of the waiting vehicle and slammed the door.

I stood where I was until I saw the car round the corner.

"Ready?" Decker asked.

"I'm sorry about what you just witnessed. He isn't usually like that."

Whatever Decker said in response, I couldn't hear, and I didn't care. It was hotter than hell, I was exhausted, an emotional wreck, and my sister was dead. Adler Livingston, for all I cared, could go fuck himself.

5

Decker

"Do you need to stop anywhere before we get on the road?" I asked once we were back in my truck and I'd started the engine.

"I don't think so."

"I should've asked when we were inside, but do you need to use the facilities?" I felt my cheeks flush, and she smiled.

"You just stood by my side while I identified my sister's body, but asking if I need to use the restroom embarrasses you?"

I turned my head and looked out the window, feeling like a jackass. "Well, do you?"

"No."

"You probably aren't hungry."

"I'm not, but if you are…"

"I'm not, either."

I backed the truck out of the parking space and got on the road.

"It'll take twenty or thirty minutes to get out there."

"I remember where it is," she said, resting her head against the seat.

"I'm gonna take the back way, if that's okay."

"You're driving, Mr. Ashford. It's up to you."

God, she was adorable, not that now was the time for me to have thoughts like that. "Name's Deck, Miss Knight."

"And my name is Mila."

I pulled out of the parking lot, and by the time we got out of town, her eyes had drifted closed.

Once I was certain Mila was asleep and wouldn't catch me, I stole several glances at the woman sitting next to me. Given what she was dealing with, the last thing I should be thinking about was how beautiful she was, or how I wanted to pull her soft body against mine and give her comfort. I couldn't help myself, though. She was breathtaking.

Her long blonde hair was pulled up in a ponytail. Not surprising in this heat. She wore a sleeveless blouse that tied at the waist and a skirt that brushed the top of her knees. Her legs were long and toned, like her arms, and the sandals she wore gave me a glimpse of her blue-painted toenails.

Her head fell forward, and I wished I had one of those neck pillows to give her so she'd be more comfortable. I didn't have as much as a damn blanket in my truck that I could roll up.

She adjusted her body, turning so she was facing me, and it was like I was struck by a lightning bolt.

I'd never known her name, but the girl who had haunted me for most of my life was sitting beside me. I'd bet my life on it. There'd never been anyone I reacted to in the same way—before or since. It had never been her looks; it had always been her soul, what I saw when I peered into her eyes.

I doubted she remembered me; we were so young at the time. The connection I felt to her from the moment I looked into her eyes at the airport made so much more sense now. It wasn't guilt over not being able to save her sister's life. This was me getting hit directly in the heart by something I couldn't explain and knowing, like I had for years, that I'd never get over it.

6

Mila

Twenty-five minutes after we left the county building, we pulled up to a gate and waited for it to open.

"There are security systems in place here at King-Alexander that I'll need to go over with you."

"Sorry, I dozed off. I feel like such an imposition."

"You're not."

He pulled up in front of a large house but didn't cut the engine. He pointed to a smaller one sitting behind it. "That's where you'll be staying, but first, we need to get you into the system."

"The system?" What was he talking about? Why did a ranch need a security system?

Decker nodded. "We can do that at my place."

He drove farther down the same road that led to the main house, and about a mile in, he turned off. The ranch didn't look any different than I remembered, not that I'd ever come inside the gates. I could tell by the number of outbuildings, though, that it was a large operation.

We came to a house similar to the one I'd be staying in and waited for the garage door to open. After he parked and climbed out, he came around to open my door.

"I wouldn't normally handle it this way, but I don't have much choice since you're already on the property," he said, leading me inside.

He opened another door just off the kitchen and stepped into what looked like an office with an elaborate surveillance system set up—the kind one might see in a movie.

"What is this place?" I mumbled, not meaning to say it out loud.

"As I said, there are security systems at the ranch—"

"Cattle ranching must be a lot different than it used to be," I commented, eyeing the number of monitors in the room.

Decker took a deep breath and let it out slowly. "It's because of who owns it." He motioned to one of the computer screens and pulled out the chair. "Come over here."

Once I was seated, he set a trackpad by the keyboard. "Put the fingertips of your right hand on this." Decker put his hand on mine and adjusted the way my fingertips rested. "Hold them like that and look right here. Keep your eyes open." He pointed to the screen. "Okay, you can relax."

He pulled out the chair, I stood, and he ushered me out of the room. After closing the door behind us, he pulled out a stool near the kitchen counter and motioned for me to take a seat there.

"We mainly use facial-recognition software here at the ranch. There are certain areas, though, where the security is more complex. It's unlikely you'll be in those areas, but just in case."

"This is not what I envisioned a ranch manager's job to be," I said, trying to lighten the seriousness of our conversation.

He smiled. "Tomorrow morning, I'll be back out on horseback, chewin' a piece of straw, and countin' head of cattle."

"Somehow, I think your life is far more complicated than that."

I motioned to the toothpick I just realized had been in his mouth since we got into the truck. "Nervous habit?"

Decker rested his arm on the back of my stool. If he leaned forward and took the toothpick out of his mouth, he could easily kiss me.

I felt my cheeks flush. *Where were these bizarre thoughts coming from?* I tried to look away, but he put his fingers on the side of my face, holding me where I was. The only thing more bizarre than my thinking—or maybe hoping—he'd kiss me, was that I hadn't flinched once when he touched me. Was it because of what he'd done years ago? Decker Ashford had been as much my hero then as he was now.

"There's something about you," he murmured.

"I make you nervous?"

"No, not nervous." As if the spell was suddenly broken, Decker walked away, stood on the opposite side of the counter, and rested his palms on the tile. "Do you want to ask me any questions?"

Are you single? No, that wouldn't be appropriate.

"You said earlier that you were the one to find my sister. Where?"

"I was on my way home late last night and found her on the side of the road."

"Was she in an accident? Was her car—"

"There was no car. Nobody around, but your sister seemed to think someone was after her."

I grasped the back of the stool hard enough that my fingernails pushed into the wood. "She was...alive?" It never occurred to me that Sybil had been found *alive*. The idea made me sick to my stomach.

Decker came back around the counter. "God, I'm sorry. I just dropped that on you. Come with me," he said, taking my hand and leading me over to the sofa.

I started to sit on the end, but he led me to the middle, sat on the coffee table in front of me, and took both my hands in his.

"What I'm about to tell you won't be easy to hear, especially today."

"Go ahead," I whispered, my eyes locked on his.

"Your sister believed someone was trying to kill her."

My eyes filled with tears. "Why?"

"I don't know. I asked who, but she wasn't able to tell me."

"Because she died?"

"Yes. She lost consciousness, and then she died."

I tried to pull my hands away, but Decker held them tight.

"I know the medical examiner said he needed to wait for the autopsy results to tell you the cause of death, but your sister died from a gunshot wound."

"Oh my God!" I gasped. "Why would anyone want to kill Sybil?"

"I was going to ask you the same thing."

I closed my eyes and thought back to the last time I was with my sister and how I'd felt as though something was wrong.

"What is it?" he asked.

"I had a bad feeling."

"When?"

"Yesterday. Last night. Before I got the call."

"Why were you worried about her?"

I shook my head. "I said I had a bad feeling."

"Again, why?"

I didn't have a reason, I just felt it. "I can't explain it. Call it intuition."

"It wasn't based on anything?"

I put my hand on my abdomen. "Do you ever get a feeling right here, in the pit of your stomach? Something so powerful that it feels like you've ingested a boulder?"

"Yes, I have."

"Then you know what I'm talking about. It doesn't have to be based on anything."

7

Decker

I knew exactly what she was talking about because it had kept me alive on many occasions.

"Mila, you should know that with any murder investigation, the victim's life, as well as that of the people close to her, is picked apart, scrutinized to the point of violation. Until law enforcement finds the answers they're seeking, they keep probing. Oftentimes, families feel as though the victim becomes the suspect."

"I understand."

"Do you? Because if there is anything about your sister's life that led to someone wanting to murder her, it will be uncovered."

"What are you suggesting?"

"They'll look into who she associated with, her finances, her employment history, even her sex life will be dissected."

Mila nodded slowly, analyzing everything I'd just said.

"Your life may be dissected as well."

"Mine? Why mine?"

"Family are usually among the first suspects. Although I guess the politically correct wording now is 'persons of interest.'" I heard my phone buzzing in the other room, not the one I left near where I'd been standing in the kitchen. This was the one in the office.

"Excuse me a minute." I stood and walked over to the door, touched the handle with the tip of my index finger, and it unlocked.

When I picked the phone up from the desk, I saw a familiar name on the screen.

"Hello, my friend," Rile said when I accepted the call after closing the office door.

"Rile."

"I just left Z's office. He got an alert that you scanned someone new into the ranch's security system."

"That's right," I said, but what I really wanted to ask was why that was any of Rile's business.

"Is there anything we can do to assist?"

"With what?"

"Your investigation."

"I'm confused, Rile. Less than twenty-four hours ago, I found a woman on the side of the road, who died a few minutes later. Today, her sister flew in to identify the body. There is no investigation."

"Yet."

"How do you know so much about it when the cause of death still hasn't been released?"

Rile chuckled. "You will find that's almost always the case."

"Are you going to clue me in?"

"When the time is right."

I didn't like the game Rile was playing one fucking bit, and I said so.

"You remain need-to-know, my friend. Sign the contract, and perhaps that will change. In the meantime, see what you can get Miss Knight to tell you about the gentleman who accompanied her to Texas."

I knew plenty already without having to ask Mila about Adler Livingston. He was an arrogant, narcissistic bastard who didn't give two shits about her.

"Decker?"

"What am I looking for?"

"Whatever you find."

I slammed the phone down on the desk after ending the call. This kind of shit was the reason I'd stayed an independent contractor as long as I did. It was also the reason I hadn't gone into intelligence full-time. Cattle never made me want to punch a hole in a wall. Well, maybe sometimes, but never as much as humans did.

"Everything okay?" Mila asked when I came back and sat on the sofa next to her.

"Tell me about your friend."

"Adler?"

"Yep."

"There isn't much to tell."

"How do you know him?"

"He's a neighbor. He lives in my building. Actually, it's the other way around. I live in his building. His family owns it."

"Are you lovers?" That probably wasn't something Rile needed to know, but I did.

Her eyes opened wide, and she stared at me.

"I warned you."

"You warned me that my sister's sex life would be scrutinized, not mine."

"So you are lovers." Even I knew I was being a dick about it, but for whatever reason, I couldn't let it go.

Her shoulders tightened. "I didn't say that."

"You also didn't say you weren't."

"It isn't any of your business."

I decided to take a different tack since Mila was obviously not willing to give me a straight answer. "What does he do?"

"For a living?"

I nodded.

"I don't really know."

"No job?"

I caught a momentary flinch, which Mila quickly masked. What was that all about?

"He manages the building."

"Maintenance? That sort of thing?"

"He hires people to do maintenance. He also travels on business from time to time."

"What about you, Miss Knight? What do you do for a living?"

"I was a music instructor."

"You aren't any longer?"

"I lost my job yesterday."

I'd circle back to that later. "How'd you meet Adler?"

"I told you, his family owns the building I live in."

"Is he friends with everyone who lives in it?"

She got up and paced to the other side of the room. "Why are you asking so many questions about Ad? He didn't even know my sister."

"Never met her?" This line of questioning was angering her. Why?

"Once, when he flew out to attend my grandfather's funeral."

I needed to call Rile back and find out exactly what kind of information he was looking for on Mila's asshole landlord. I wasn't making any headway other than to piss her off.

"I don't want to be rude, but I'm really tired. I didn't get much sleep last night, and then the flight…"

"Right."

"Would you mind taking me to the guest house now? I'd like to get some rest."

I stood to pick up my keys. There was something about this that didn't feel right. The more she talked, the more I felt it.

"I changed my mind. I think you should stay here." I pointed toward the hallway. "I have a guest room."

"Why?"

"Did I change my mind?"

Mila nodded, and I pointed to my gut. "Call it intuition."

8

Adler

"What in the hell do you mean, she's in Texas and you're back in Boston?" my father, Marshall, barked.

"She wanted to stay a few more days. I told her she needed to come back with me, but she refused."

I heard the phone drop and a muffled conversation in the background, followed by the sound of my dad picking the phone back up.

"You have one job, one responsibility. You stick to Mila Knight like fucking glue. Do you understand me?" he yelled.

"She isn't going to agree to come back here. At least not right away."

"Then you get your ass on the next plane back to Texas!"

9

Mila

I was too strung out to argue with Decker. Plus, I was a guest. I could hardly demand where I stayed.

"Bathroom is across the hall," he said after showing me the bedroom. He pointed to a door in the bathroom. "Whatever you need in the way of towels is in this closet. Get some rest," he added before walking away.

The sun was still high enough in the sky that when I looked out the bedroom window, I could see the rolling hills of the ranch along with cattle scattered on them. I'd heard rumors about this ranch all my life but had never been on the property before. It was as impressive as I'd always heard, but then the King name alone was synonymous with the biggest and best in Texas, maybe in all of the US.

I lay on the queen-size bed and closed my eyes, trying to remember everything I could about the last time I saw my sister.

While we'd argued from the time we were kids, our last argument was about money. When I suggested Sybil get a job to pay for the upkeep of the house in Bluebell

Creek, I got a lengthy dressing down about how she'd put her life on hold to care for our dying grandfather while I enjoyed my fancy life in Boston.

For the last four years, Adler had played a significant role in the life my sister referred to as fancy. Decker's questions about him had unnerved me. He'd excused himself to take a call, and when he came back, he'd immediately launched into what felt like an interrogation about my relationship with Adler. Granted, he'd behaved like an asshole when we were leaving the county building. Never, in the four years I'd known him, had he behaved as rudely as he did this morning. It was obvious Decker annoyed him, but that didn't explain why Adler was rude to me, or so demanding. He was usually easy-going, eager to do whatever I wanted to do, even when it was nothing.

Still, out of all the questions Decker could've asked, why was the second one whether we were lovers?

I took several deep breaths, trying to calm my racing heart. The last twenty-four hours had been a nightmare. Just learning my sister was dead and having to look at her lifeless body was the worst thing I could imagine.

Finding out that Sybil believed someone was trying to kill her—did kill her, according to Decker—was more than I could wrap my head around. Adding Adler and his bizarre behavior into the mix was something I couldn't begin to process.

I sat on the edge of the bed, wishing I had my guitar. Playing piano was my preference when I was feeling stressed, but my apartment wasn't big enough for me to have one, not that I would've been able to afford a piano. There were practice rooms I could use at school, and at this time of year, they were mostly empty. Those days were over, though. The college wasn't renewing my contract, which meant no more practice rooms, no more paychecks, and no more apartment in Boston. With my savings depleted, I needed to come up with a way to support myself, and I had to do it quickly.

I was about to change my clothes when I heard a knock at the door. I opened it and looked up into Decker's piercing green eyes. I'd seen nothing but kindness and concern in them.

"I'm making dinner."

"Thanks, but I'm really not hungry."

"If you change your mind, you know where the kitchen is." He walked back down the hallway, and I closed the door.

After getting more comfortable clothes out of my carry on and changing, I lay down on the bed and closed my eyes. Soon, the smells wafting from the kitchen made my stomach rumble. I had no idea what Decker was cooking, but it smelled heavenly.

He looked up when I came out to join him.

"It smells too good to resist," I admitted.

"I made enough for two."

"What is it?"

"Chile relleno," he said, opening the oven door. "Hope you like spicy."

"I love it."

The man smiled again, and I felt it from my head to my toes. He was a typical cowboy. Not only was he a Wrangler-, pearl snap-, and boot-wearing man, he was built like someone who spent his days on the back of a horse—all hard edges and calloused hands. He talked like a cowboy, acted like a cowboy, and worse, looked like a cowboy. A real man—not someone who spent his life sleeping the days away or with his nose in a book. Although, there was a well-stocked bookcase in his living room.

He reminded me of my mother's father. My grandfather had been gruff with the same cocky arrogance, but underneath it all, I'd known I could depend on him.

I felt the same way about Decker. It didn't matter that as far as he was concerned, we'd just met, it was the feeling I got from him—he'd watch over and protect me. I could depend on Decker Ashford in a way I now knew I could never depend on Adler.

"I don't know what you were thinking, but it was nice to see the glimmer of a smile on your face, however briefly."

With his mention of it, I smiled again. He pulled the pan of steaming food out of the oven and set it on the counter.

"What can I do to help?"

"Plates are in the cabinet next to the oven, silverware in that drawer."

While I collected the things he mentioned, Decker put two placemats on the counter and took two beers out of the refrigerator. He held one up. "You in?"

"Sure, thanks," I answered, taking the bottle from his outstretched hand. When our fingers brushed, I shook my head.

"Why'd you shake your head?" he asked, spooning the chile into two bowls.

I took a deep breath, knowing that what I was about to say would likely lead to questions I didn't want to answer. "I don't like to be touched."

He took a slight step back and raised his hands. "Whoa. I'll be more careful not to touch you."

"That isn't why I shook my head."

He put one bowl in front of me and then grabbed the other and sat down. "Why, then?"

"It doesn't bother me as much when you do it." It made no sense, even to me. Or especially to me. What was normally a visceral reaction, simply didn't happen with him.

"That's what all women say about me. It doesn't bother them *as much* when I touch them."

He didn't even try to hide his smile, which made me smile too.

"Somehow, I doubt you have any trouble with women."

Decker reached over and brushed his pinky finger against mine. "It's because of my soft touch."

I rolled my eyes, plunged my fork into the chile, and blew on it. "It smells so good I almost can't wait to take a bite."

The look on his face changed; heat emanated from his eyes. "I feel the same way."

My breathing accelerated, and I tried to look away, but he captivated me.

"Take a bite, Mila. I won't until you do."

10

Decker

Between the heat of the chilies and that of the woman sitting beside me, I wanted to open the refrigerator and crawl inside. Maybe the freezer would work better. Except I couldn't move at the moment. If I did, there'd be no hiding the fact that my jeans were growing snug in the crotch.

I'd almost choked on the glass of water I was drinking when she walked into the kitchen a few minutes ago wearing thin, little shorts and a top that looked more like lingerie than something she should be wearing in public—and given she hadn't known me twenty-four hours, she should consider me public.

I took another forkful of chilies and did my damnedest to drown out the sounds she was making with every bite she took. I sneaked a peek, and damn if from this angle, I couldn't see the swell of her perfect breasts or the way her nipples were puckering in the chill of the air conditioning. Add her mewls of pleasure over the food I cooked, and I found myself needing to adjust my jeans.

As awkward as it was, I slid from the stool with my back to her. I gingerly made my way around the counter, wishing for the first time in my life that I was shorter.

"Are you okay?"

I looked up. "Yeah. Why?"

"You look like you're in pain."

"I'm fine," I answered, doing my best to avert my eyes from the nipples that were now pointing directly at me.

I heard the ringtone of a phone, but it wasn't one of mine.

"Sorry, it's Adler," she said, climbing off the stool to go into the bedroom.

I wished I had monitoring devices set up in the guest room so I could hear what they were talking about. I didn't want to think too hard about what kind of sleazeball that made me as I walked over to take my seat at the counter. I took another bite of my dinner and was happy to see the door open and Mila come back out. What I didn't like was the look on her face.

"Everything okay?"

She shook her head and looked up at me. "He wants to come back."

"When?"

"Tomorrow morning, and before you ask, he wouldn't tell me why he had a change of heart."

"What did you tell him?"

"Obviously, I told him not to come."

"And?"

"He said he's coming anyway."

"I see." Knowing I was about to say something I shouldn't about the asshole, I got up to get another beer. Mila sat on the stool and jabbed her fork into her dinner. "Want another?" I asked.

"Sure, thanks," she said, downing what was left in the first bottle.

I came back around and sat down. "When does he arrive?"

"I don't know."

I wanted to ask ten questions all at once. Was this asshole planning on coming to the ranch? Did Mila expect me to offer to let him stay here with her? I already knew the answer to that one if she did—no way in hell.

She looked over at me sheepishly, and I tensed, waiting for what she'd say next. "I...um...kind of told him that he wouldn't be able to see me if he came against my wishes."

Good girl, I wanted to shout.

"I also told him the ranch had an elaborate security system and that he wouldn't be able to get in."

"True statement."

"You're not upset?"

I turned to look at her. "Why would I be?"

"All the drama. You picked me up at the airport and probably didn't intend to see me again after you dropped me off at the sheriff's office. Here it is several hours later, and not only am I still with you, you have to deal with my shitty life too."

When she leaned against the back of the stool, I leaned forward, putting my arm around her back. "I like having you here," I murmured, my mouth as close to her ear as I could get it.

"You're strange," she said with a nervous laugh.

"And you're intriguing."

Even though I told her she didn't have to, Mila insisted on helping me clean up. By the time we were finished, she looked as though she was about to collapse.

"Go get some rest," I said, walking her down the hallway.

Mila put her hand on the bedroom doorknob but didn't open it. She turned around and looked into my eyes. "Thank you for everything you did for me today," she said. "You're a good man, Decker."

I stood outside the bedroom after the door closed, wondering if she'd think the same thing about me if she knew the raging hard-on I now sported for her.

It had been a long damn time since I was unable to control my libido around a woman, but with her, my need was almost constant. It made me feel like a pervert.

The next morning, I was up before dawn, like I always was, and getting ready to leave the house when the guest room door opened. "You're up early," I commented, looking at my phone rather than at her. She still wore the tiny shorts and that top, and her hair was loose around her face. She looked exactly the way I'd dreamed about last night when I let myself imagine what it would be like to sink into her soft body. Except in my dream, she was naked. My eyes rolled back in my head just thinking about it.

"I couldn't sleep," she murmured. "Are you leaving?"

I'd planned to get to the barn and back before she woke up, but since she was awake, I'd send my barn manager a text, letting him know to carry on without me.

"Morning chores, but no, I'm not leaving. Is there something you wanted to do today? Somewhere you wanted to go?"

Mila looked at the floor. "I don't know what I'm supposed to do, Decker."

"What do you want to do?"

"I don't know." Before going into the bathroom and closing the door behind her, Mila sighed. She looked sad, but there was something more. She seemed defeated.

I went into my office to see if Rile had answered my email about Adler, but there was no response so far. When I went back into the kitchen, Mila was standing near the counter, looking off into space.

"Can I get you anything?"

"No," she said, turning to walk away.

"Wait."

She stopped but didn't turn back.

"What were you looking for?"

"Coffee, but it isn't a big deal. I can go back to my room."

I walked over to where she stood and put my hand on her shoulder. "Look at me, beautiful."

Mila shook her head, and I walked around her so I could see her face. I cupped her cheek, and she looked into my eyes.

"I'm lost," she whispered. Tears ran down her cheeks, and she bowed her head.

I put one hand around her waist and the other behind her knees, picked her up, carried her over to the sofa, and sat down with her on my lap.

"You had a helluva day yesterday, sweetheart."

It was as if once I gave her permission to accept how hard the last thirty-six hours had been for her, the floodgates opened. The shock had finally worn off, and Mila let herself cry. I held her as tight as I could, giving her the space and time she needed to sob over the death of her sister.

I soothed her the best I could, and when she apologized for crying, I told her to let it out. "Don't apologize, Mila. You haven't let herself do this, and you need to." That seemed to make her cry harder, but that was okay. I'd meant what I said. This was something she needed to do.

I had no idea how much time had passed when her sobs finally subsided. She took several deep breaths, wrapped her arm around my waist, shifted the way she sat on my lap, and rested her head against my chest. As far as I was concerned, there wasn't a better feeling in the world. At least none I could allow myself to think about with her ass firmly planted where my erection was currently coming to life.

"Tell you what. Let's get out of here today, maybe take a drive somewhere."

"You don't have to work?"

I shook my head. "It's called delegation, and I'm damn good at it."

"Where would we go?"

"I don't know. Maybe head down to San Antonio, take a walk along the river."

Her eyes lit up like she thought it was a good idea. "I have someplace else in mind."

Oh. Not such a good idea. As long as she didn't say the fucking airport to meet asshole Adler, I didn't care where she wanted to go; I'd take her.

"I know you said we couldn't get into my grandfather's house, where my sister was living, but I grew up in Bluebell Creek. It's where my granddaddy and my mama are both buried. I need to make arrangements for Sybil too."

"You don't have to do that today."

"I know, but I love that little town."

"If that's where you'd like to go, I may have a place where you can stay."

"Really? I'd appreciate it."

"Bluebell Creek it is," I said, moving her off my lap and then wondering why I'd been so anxious to do so. Seconds after she stood, I wanted her back in my arms and to never let her go. "Do you want some breakfast before we head out?" I asked, standing and quickly adjusting my jeans.

Mila was already halfway down the hallway.

"Just coffee, and a shower if that's okay."

"Take your time, sweetheart. We've got all day."

When I looked up, her smile almost knocked me on my ass.

"Thank you, Decker."

"For?"

"Making me feel like you care about me. I haven't felt that for a long time."

I wanted to ask why she didn't feel that way about Adler, but it would've only been to hear her tell me why not. And that would've only been to stroke my ego. It didn't matter, though; she was already in the bathroom with the door closed.

An hour later, we were on our way to the small town that was a four-hour drive from the King-Alexander Ranch. It hadn't taken thirty minutes before she fell asleep.

Her head bobbed, reminding me about wishing I'd had a pillow of some kind she could rest her head against yesterday.

When we got to the next town, I'd stop if I saw a drugstore, and run in and get something. Twenty minutes later, I pulled into a parking lot.

"Where are we?" she asked, sitting up.

"Quick stop. Can I get you anything? Do you want to come in?"

"I'll wait here if that's okay. And water would be nice. Thank you."

It didn't take me long to find what I was looking for. On my way out, I grabbed a cheap cooler to throw some drinks in. The temperature was over the one-hundred-degree mark today, and we needed to stay hydrated. Before walking back outside, I sent a quick text to my barn manager, letting him know I wasn't sure when I'd be back.

The man answered quickly with a thumbs up.

"Here," I said, handing Mila the pillow. "Thought you'd be more comfortable."

"You didn't have to do that, but thank you," she said, not hesitating to rest her head against it.

"Go back to sleep," I told her once we were on the road and I noticed her fighting it again.

"I'm sorry. I can't keep my eyes open."

"Nothing to apologize for. You need the rest."

By the time we got to Waco, it was mid-morning and my stomach was rumbling. I hoped she wouldn't mind if I stopped to get a quick bite to eat, but first, I needed to gas up the truck.

"Where are we?" she asked like she had before.

"Waco. I'll just pick up something quick to eat, and we'll get back on the road."

"I could eat," she said, stretching her arms over her head and exposing her bare midriff. I couldn't stop myself from looking. When I raised my eyes, it was obvious she'd caught me.

I wasn't sure whether I should apologize, until I saw the heat in her eyes. Miss Knight hadn't minded my gaze on her, one bit.

Under other circumstances, I'd reach across the console and kiss the shit out of her. But these weren't other circumstances.

"There's the silo place that those fixer-upper people built," I said, figuring most women would want to see it.

"I'm fine if we go somewhere less like a theme park. Although, again, you're driving."

My shoulders dropped in relief. I rolled down both of our windows and hopped out to pump the gas. When I got back in the truck, Mila had her phone out. Was she texting Adler to see if he came after all? I hated how the idea that she was made me feel. I wasn't sure what to do when she handed me her phone.

"You may already know of a place, but here are some options," she told me.

"First one sounds good," I said, handing the phone back to her. I pulled out onto the road and saw it was two blocks down.

"What are you hungry for?" I asked once we were seated and the waitress brought over menus.

"Just some toast," she said, not looking up at me.

"We can leave if you don't want to be here," I offered.

Her eyes met mine. "I'm okay. I just...it's..."

"You don't need to explain."

I perused the menu, and when I raised my head, Mila was looking out the window. The way the sun hit her blonde hair, she looked like an angel.

The waitress approached the table, and Mila turned her head, breaking the spell she'd had me under.

"Are you okay?" she asked when the waitress left the table.

"Yeah, I'm fine."

She cocked her head briefly and then looked back out the window. Neither of us spoke again until after our food arrived.

"How long have you lived in Boston?" I asked between forkfuls of pancakes.

"Since college, so almost eight years."

"You like it there?"

Mila shrugged. "Better than here." Her cheeks turned pink. "Sorry. No offense."

"None taken. Were you born in Texas?"

"Yes, sir," she answered, exaggerating her accent and rolling her eyes. "I'm Texan through and through." She shook her head. "Sorry. Again. I just..."

I wiped my mouth with my napkin and sat back. I liked that she was being playful. "Just what?"

"I wanted a change."

Change was understandable, but why Boston? "Not all that uncommon. Boston is a big one."

"You've been?" she asked, picking up her last piece of toast.

"Yes, ma'am," I answered, smiling at her slight and handing it right back to her. "Every once in a while, they let us good ol' boys out explorin'."

The smile left her face. "You must think I'm a raving bitch."

"Nothing wrong with wanting a change. Nothing wrong with wanting to start your life over." I'd certainly wanted to when I was younger, much younger than she was when she left Texas, though.

"Are you from Texas originally?"

I caught my flinch, hoping Mila didn't pick up on it. "New Mexico, actually, but I only lived there a couple of years."

"Then your family moved to Texas?"

"Something like that."

"Sorry. I'm prying."

I looked at her empty plate and the way she was eyeing my last pancake. "You still hungry?"

"I'll be okay."

"That isn't the answer to the question I asked," I said, moving her plate out of the way and pushing mine over in front of her.

"I can't eat your food."

I motioned for the waitress, who was at a table nearby.

"What else can I get ya, sugar?" she asked with a wink.

"Another side of pancakes." I looked at Mila. "Anything else?"

Her cheeks turned pink again and she started to push the plate back toward me. "I'm fine."

I stopped it with my hand. "Two more sides of pancakes, please." I didn't look up at the woman; I kept my gaze on Mila long after the waitress had walked away.

"Thanks," she said, finally taking a bite of the food in front of her. "I'm hungrier than I thought I was."

"So why Boston?"

"It's where I wanted to go to school."

"You said you were a music teacher?"

"Instructor—or at least, I was—at Northeastern College of Music, where I got my degree."

I envied the male students in her classes. If I got to look up at her pretty face every day, not to mention her rockin' body, I would've taken every class she taught. "What did you teach?"

"Music theory, critical listening, piano. I was supposed to teach copyright law next semester."

"Impressive," I said, digging into my now-cold eggs. She shrugged. "Did you…"

I looked up. "Go to college?"

Her cheeks were flushed. She gave a slight nod and looked away.

"You're even prettier when you're embarrassed."

Her head snapped back in my direction; she opened her mouth and then closed it.

"I'm not sure how it works in the big city, but here in Texas, when a man gives a woman a compliment, it's customary for the woman to say thank you." I winked.

Before she had a chance to respond, my phone buzzed. I looked at the screen and saw it was Mac calling. "Excuse me. I need to take this." I got up from the table and walked out the front door. The heat engulfed me like a cocoon. Damn Texas summers.

"Anything to tell me?"

"Afraid so. The sister's place was trashed. Somebody was lookin' for somethin'."

"Any signs that whoever killed her started the process there?"

"None so far. Neighbors told one of our deputies that her car was parked in a back parking lot. That was trashed too."

Shit, this was getting uglier. As Mac said, someone was looking for something. Would whoever it was come after Mila next? "Let me know if you find out anything else."

I went back to the table. "Sorry I disappeared on you." I must've been gone longer than I thought. There was a plate of pancakes on my side of the table, and Mila looked like she was almost finished with hers.

"I'll take these to go," I told the waitress when she stopped back by to drop off the check. Mila and I reached for it at the same time.

"Please let me get it. You've done so much for me already."

I wasn't accustomed to letting a woman pick up the check, but something in her eyes made me relent.

"Thank you, Mila."

For a moment, I thought I'd done the wrong thing based on the look on her face. Before I could speak, she got up and walked over to where the cash register sat on the counter.

I waited for the waitress to bring my to-go box, and then stood to join her.

"There must be some mistake," I heard her say when the kid at the register handed her back her credit card.

"Sorry, ma'am. It was declined."

While she rummaged through her purse, probably looking for cash, I quietly slid a fifty-dollar bill in the kid's direction.

She looked up when he handed me the change.

"I'm mortified," she said when we got back out to the truck.

"Maybe you should give 'em a call. Sometimes they decline a card if someone's traveling."

She nodded but didn't take out her phone.

11

Mila

There was a very slim chance that Decker was right. There was a much larger chance that I was over my limit. If that was the case, I couldn't bear the embarrassment of having the conversation with my bank in such close proximity to him.

He started the engine, but didn't put the truck in gear.

"It's been a hard year," I said, looking out the passenger window, too embarrassed to look directly at him.

"You don't owe me any explanation."

I shook my head. The man had been so incredibly nice to me, but he wasn't interested in hearing the sob stories of what my life had been like. "Right." I closed my eyes, willing the tears filling them to dry up in the Texas heat.

"Mila, look at me," I heard him murmur, and slowly turned my head. "I got some more bad news earlier."

I waited for him to continue, mesmerized by the kindness I saw once again in his green eyes.

"The place where your sister was living, did you say it was your grandfather's house?"

"That's right."

"Someone broke in and trashed the place. They were obviously looking for something. Do you have any idea what it might be?"

What in the hell had Sybil gotten herself into? Every worry and fear I'd had in the last two months were suddenly justified. Yet, the truth was, my sister and I had never been close. I knew little to nothing about her life. I shook my head.

"If I remember correctly, you said your grandfather passed earlier this year."

"In January."

"Were you in contact with your sister since that time?"

"Yes. I mean, we didn't talk often, but I was taking care of my grandfather's debts, so I heard from her when she received statements."

"Was your sister working?"

"Not that I'm aware of." When my eyes filled with tears again, I looked away from him.

Decker reached over and covered my hand with his. "We'll get to the bottom of this, I promise. We'll find out who killed her."

"Thank you," I whispered, looking back at him. "You're so kind to me. I can't—" Why did I have to keep dissolving into tears?

He reached out and brushed a tear away. "I made you a promise, and I'm going to keep it. Understand?"

I stared into his eyes, wondering why I was putting so much trust in a man who was practically a stranger. I'd seen him one time in my life prior to this: when I was a child. It wasn't logical that I'd feel this comfortable around him based solely on that. The only answer I could come up with was that I didn't see what other choice I had.

"Want to see one of my favorite places in Bluebell Creek?"

I smiled. "Sure."

Decker took a deep breath. "I sure like seeing you smile, Mila."

His lips were close enough that if I leaned forward just a little bit, I could kiss him. I wanted to so badly, but what would he think of me? What kind of woman would that make me in his eyes? A virtual stranger whose sister had just died, kissing him? He'd probably turn around, drive back to Austin, and put me on the next flight to Boston just to get rid of me.

"I don't know what you're thinking," he said, brushing my bottom lip with his finger, "but I want you to know you can trust me."

"I do trust you."

"I hope this doesn't make you change your mind."

When Decker leaned forward and brushed my lips with his, it was as if every wall I'd erected around myself over the last few years came crumbling down. When he traced my lips with his tongue, I opened to him and then wrapped my arms around his neck. I deepened our kiss, not Decker, and when I felt him pulling away, I was mortified by how aggressive I'd been.

"Hey, now," he murmured, stroking my cheek with his finger.

"I'm sorry, I don't know what came over me." I tried to back away, but Decker's grip on me tightened.

"I hope the same thing came over you that came over me, sweetheart."

My cheeks flushed, and I tried to look away from him. I brought my fingertips to my lips. No one had ever kissed me the way Deck just did.

"Do you know that I've wanted to do that since the first moment I laid eyes on you?"

"You have?"

He brought his lips to mine again. As our tongues wound around each other's, a need started to build from deep inside me. How long had I wondered if I'd ever experience desire, if I'd ever be able to react to a man with anything but fear?

Decker pulled back and looked into my eyes. "I wish I knew what you were thinking."

"Maybe I'm thinking the same thing you are."

"I have to admit, I'm thinking about how nice it would be to feel your body against mine."

"Same," I answered, hoping that if and when the time came for that to happen, I wouldn't freeze up or find myself unable to go through with it.

Decker put the truck in gear, and soon, we were back out on a road that was very familiar to me. While my mama had been from Bluebell Creek, my daddy hailed from Austin. I remembered when I was a little girl, my parents, my sister, and I would drive this same route to visit my granddaddy.

Once my parents divorced, we moved in with him. We rarely saw my father after that, and the last time I did, was one of the worst days of my life.

Decker put his hand on my arm, startling me. "You okay?" he asked.

I nodded. "Just thinkin' about my parents."

"You keep in touch with Judd?"

Judd. God, I'd forgotten that's what people called him. "Do you know him?"

"Only met him once or twice. He came to the ranch to meet with Z."

"Quint's daddy?"

Decker nodded. "I think they were friends, although I'm pretty sure he was better friends with Wasp."

"Wasp King. That's a name I haven't heard for a long time."

"I never met him."

I hadn't either, but I remembered hearing stories about him.

"You didn't answer me," said Decker, sliding his fingers from my hand to my knee. "About Judd."

"We lost touch."

"I wondered, when you said you paid your grand-daddy's debts. I'm surprised Judd didn't step in and take care of it."

Decker didn't know the half of how accurate his statement was. Judd Knight took care of himself. No one else.

"Not everybody's cut out to be a parent," I murmured.

12

Decker

Didn't I know it. Neither of mine were, that was for damn sure. I was in single digits when they split up, and unlike Mila's, my mama didn't stick around to take care of me, and neither did my daddy.

Child Protective Services did, though. Not that they did much protecting. Up until the time I met Quint Alexander, I'd been bounced from one abusive situation to another.

When I was thirteen, Z approached me. I guessed he'd caught glimpses of the bruises that dotted my body.

"Would you like to live here with us?" Z had asked.

I hadn't known what to say. "Can I?" I remember asking. After that day, I didn't go back to the house I'd been living in, not even to get my belongings, which were meager.

I looked over at Mila, who was as lost in thought as I was. "The place I'm taking you is on the outskirts of town. You okay with that?"

Mila sighed. "The truth is, Decker, I've really got no place to be except here with you."

I squeezed her hand. Damn if I didn't like the sound of that more than I should. As soon as I was able to figure out who killed her sister, Mila Knight would be on the first plane back to Boston, and probably into the arms of the asshole. I was more attracted to her than I remember being to any other woman, but that didn't mean I couldn't keep myself in check.

It wasn't long before we came to the turnoff that would take us to the cabin that sat on the edge of Bluebell Creek. It had belonged to members of the King family up until recently when Quint approached them about buying it and they'd agreed.

I knew damn well why the cabin meant so much to my best friend; it held some pretty special memories for him and the woman who was now Quint's wife.

"It's so beautiful," Mila said when I drove up to the log structure. "Like out of a book."

The whole place was surrounded by wildflowers, and the sun shining through the trees lit the place up like a photograph.

I walked up to the front door, reached above it, and felt for the key. I blew the dust from it and slid it into the lock.

The cabin smelled as musty as I expected it to. However, with all the windows covered, it was cool inside.

When I turned around, Mila had a handful of flowers and was filling a pitcher that she'd found near the sink with water.

"Pretty," I said, looking at her rather than the flowers.

"You're good for my ego," she said, setting the flowers on the table.

I walked over to where she stood. "No ego stroking, Mila. You're beautiful."

"What can I do?" she asked, brushing dust from her hands.

"I thought I'd get the place opened up."

I went in to open up the windows in the bedrooms while Mila opened the ones in the kitchen and great room.

"I'd love to take a walk by the creek if you're up for it," she said when I came back out.

We'd been walking for at least a half hour when we came to an old stone bridge.

"I need a photo of this," she said, pulling out her phone. She swiped the screen and frowned.

"What?" I asked.

"Who."

"Adler?"

Mila nodded. "He's livid."

I held my breath, waiting for what she'd do next. Would she ask me to take her back? Call him? Maybe send him a text, apologizing?

She did none of those things. I watched as she took two photos of the bridge and then turned the phone in my direction. "Would you mind?" she asked.

"Taking a photo of you? Never."

She shook her head. "I was thinking of us. Is that too weird?" She shook her head again. "Me and the guy who found my dead sister," she added, mumbling.

I took the phone from her hand and drew her into me. "I hope you can think of me as someone more than that."

"I do. I'm sorry I said that. I just wonder…what you must think of me."

"Hmm. If I recall correctly, it wasn't that long ago that I told you you were beautiful. I also told you that I wanted to kiss you from the first moment I saw you."

When she smiled but looked away, I put my fingers on her cheek. "Look at me," I murmured. "I understand, Mila. Yes, what brought us together was tragic. But along with wanting to kiss you, I knew from the minute I heard your voice, looked into your eyes, that you were someone special. That you'd be someone special to me." What I didn't say was that the first time I looked into those eyes, hadn't been two days ago. It was years ago, but even then, I'd known.

When I kissed her again, she relaxed into me. Her body felt like heaven up against mine. I held the phone up and took a photo, hoping that I'd gotten us in the frame since I didn't break our kiss to do it.

"Take another one," she said, resting her head against my chest and smiling.

I looked at the image, tapped the screen, and sent it to myself. "I've been meaning to tell you to put my number in your phone. Now you have it."

I was just about to hand it back to her when I saw a message flash on the screen from Adler.

I'm frantic, it read. *I'm sorry for the way I acted. Please tell me where you are and that you're safe.*

I didn't know what the other messages from him said, but I had to empathize with the guy. If Mila had ghosted me, I'd be frantic too. I watched as she read the same message I had.

"Would you mind?" she asked like she had earlier about taking a photo.

"Not at all. I'll be on the bridge—"

Before I could walk away, Mila put her hand on my arm. "Please stay."

I nodded, hating that I was close enough to hear the man's voice, but relieved that I'd know what they were saying to each other.

"Hi," she said when Adler answered almost immediately.

"Where are you?"

"In Bluebell Creek...um...it's where my mother and grandfather are buried."

"Yes, I remember. I was there with you. I'll be there in...however long it'll take me to get there. Are you at the cemetery now?"

"No!" she answered and then softened her tone. "I'd rather you not come, Ad. I'm fine. I'm sorry you flew all the way here, but please, just go home. I'll be in touch."

"I'm on my way, Mil. I'll be there as soon as I can."

I could hear the chime of the call ending. Mila stared at the screen, put the phone in her back pocket, and then took it out again and powered it off.

"I guess I didn't handle that very well," she said.

"I'm not sure what you could've done or said differently."

"He isn't very good at taking no for an answer."

I felt my shoulders tightening and didn't doubt my anger was evident on my face. "Do you want to elaborate?"

"Not in the way you might be thinking. I know I never gave you a straight answer, but Adler and I are just friends. He flirts but knows that I'm not interested in anything more than what we have." She stopped talking, but it seemed to me like there was something else she wanted to say. When she didn't continue, I led her over to the bridge, feeling inexplicably relieved that she and the asshole hadn't had sex.

As we sat on the stone and watched the water trickling over the slate beneath us, Mila looked everywhere but at me.

"There are some things...I thought maybe I was making too much of, but..."

"Go on."

"The night I got the call about Sybil, earlier that day, when I came home from work, Adler picked up my mail for me. I'm not always crazy about him having a key to my place, but I understand why he does. The mail, though. It bothered me."

"Rightly so. The key should bother you too."

"And then yesterday...I've never seen him act the way he did. It seemed like maybe there was something else going on that was bothering him."

I had a theory, but I was more interested in what Mila would say.

"He was on his phone. I know it sounds like I'm making more of it than I should, but he never does that when he's with me. I'm probably being petty. I mean, he has a life outside of his friendship with me."

"You said you've known him since you rented the apartment. How long have you lived there?"

"Four years."

"And how long before the two of you became friends?"

"It was immediate. He started out checking to see if I needed anything, welcoming me to the building, and then he just started hanging out."

"How did you find the place?"

Mila thought it over. "I don't remember. Probably a flyer at the college."

Something nagged at me, but until I had a chance to look into this guy's background further, I wouldn't ask Mila any more questions. Except for one.

"What's next with him? How do you see this playing out?"

"If you're talking about him driving up to Bluebell Creek, I have no idea. I didn't agree to meet him anywhere, so I guess when he gets here, I'll have to talk to him again." Mila turned to me. "Unless you think I should meet him. I mean, he could probably help me find a place to stay so I'm not putting you out."

I peered into her eyes long enough that her cheeks turned pink.

"What?" she said, trying to move out of my line of sight.

I wouldn't let her, though. I cupped her cheek with my palm. "I'll just say this...not a chance in hell."

She laughed, but I didn't do as much as crack a smile.

"I'm not joking."

"Okay," she murmured. "I didn't mean to make you mad."

"I have a proposition for you."

"Okay," she repeated.

"Let's go into town now, pick up some groceries, and come back here."

"I'm with you so far."

"Tomorrow we'll visit the cemetery."

"What about Adler?"

I hadn't quite figured that out yet, but a plan was beginning to formulate.

13

Mila

I shook my hands in an attempt to get them to stop trembling. Why was I so nervous? It was like I was a child about to get in trouble for skipping out of school and I knew that, at any moment, my mother was going to catch me. It was ridiculous. There was no way Adler could get to Bluebell Creek in the time it had taken us to go to the grocery store. Besides, I'd told him not to come, and I'd also told him to leave. Why should I feel guilty over not arranging for a place for us to meet?

Sitting in the coffee shop next door to the market, I waited for Decker, who said he wanted to make a couple of phone calls before we returned to the cabin.

I was flooded with relief when I saw him walk in. The feeling quickly went away when I saw the look on his face.

"Is everything okay?" I asked when he sat across from me in the booth.

"Everything is fine." He looked over his shoulder and motioned to the waitress.

"You must not play very much poker."

His eyes met mine.

"You have a terrible poker face, Decker."

"Problems at the ranch. Nothing that concerns you," he said, but before he spoke, he looked away from me.

"What can I get you, darlin'?" asked the waitress, looking straight at Decker.

"Did you order anything?" he asked me.

"Not yet." I didn't bother telling him that until he walked in, the waitress hadn't acknowledged my presence. I couldn't really blame the woman; Decker was one of the hottest men I'd ever seen too, even if I was pissed at him at the moment for just dismissing me.

"I was thinking a piece of pie. Does that sound good?" he asked.

"We've got blueberry, apple, and there may be one slice of strawberry left. I'll have to check."

Decker looked up at the waitress until she finally got a clue that was what he wanted her to do.

"Any of those sound good?"

I shook my head. "I'm suddenly not hungry."

He got up, took my hand, led me out of the coffee shop, and over to where he'd parked the truck. "Let's get on the road."

"Are you going to tell me what's going on?"

He didn't answer right away, and I didn't climb into the truck. If it was something he couldn't tell me, then he should say so, not lie and say it didn't concern me. I folded my arms.

"Yes," he finally said with a sigh.

By the time we got back to the cabin, my irritation was skyrocketing.

He pulled up, turned off the engine, but didn't make a move to get out.

"You've probably picked up on the fact that I do a little more than manage King-Alexander Ranch."

"Yes," I responded, my arms still folded in front of me.

"There's a group of guys I'm...working with...that I...um...have asked to step in and give a hand with the investigation."

He turned and looked at me as if to see if that was enough of an answer. I kept my eyes focused on his.

"Shit," I heard him mutter after he turned his head away from me and then back. "I asked them to take a deeper look into your friend's background."

"Adler's?"

"That's right."

"Did you think that would upset me?"

"Would you mind if we went inside?"

"Not at all." I climbed out before he had a chance to come around and open the door. Decker grabbed a few of the grocery bags, and I brought the rest, smiling that he'd made sure to leave me the lighter ones.

We unpacked the food we'd bought; I put some of it in the refrigerator and left the non-perishable stuff on the counter. I must've been hungry while we were shopping because now that I wasn't, it looked like we bought enough food to last several days.

"You haven't answered me," I reminded him when the last of the food was put away and I'd opened a bottle of wine. "Would you like a glass?" I asked.

Decker held up a bottle of beer that he'd pulled out of the refrigerator.

"Not a wine drinker?"

"No, I like wine," he said before he took a big swig of beer.

I went out and sat on the porch; Decker followed and sat next to me, close enough that our legs and arms were touching.

"It's a yes or no answer, Decker."

He took another big drink. "Actually, it isn't."

I set my glass of wine on the table and turned my body so I could look at him.

He took a deep breath. "The night that I found your sister, I was on my way home from the airport after flying back from England."

I had no idea what this had to do with my being upset or not about his looking into Adler's background, but it was obvious that whatever Decker was about to tell me was somehow relevant.

"I had traveled there for…other reasons."

I smiled.

"A consulting job. Anyway, while I was there, I was approached by a man about a startup company he wants me to be part of. That's who I called."

"I'm being patient, Decker, but I wish you'd connect these dots for me."

"I'm getting there," he said, standing. "Be right back."

He came back with another beer for himself along with the bottle of wine. I took a sip, and then he poured some more before he sat back down.

"I do work in the intelligence field." He looked at me again as if to gauge my reaction.

"I never would've guessed, given the spy-central setup in your house."

He smiled. "That's the side I'm on. Technology. I got into it because of Z Alexander. He saw something in me when I was a kid, and he nurtured it."

"I take it intelligence is Z's field too."

"I'm not giving away any of England's national secrets by telling you Z is the head of MI6. It's information you could easily get from their website. Anyway, these guys, they're MI6 too. Actually, two of them are MI5 agents, but that's not the point."

"What is the point?"

"I've always been an independent contractor. There are times, like calving and branding season, that I just can't be away from the ranch. That, and you may have noticed I don't always play well with others. I may have been accused of being a little gruff from time to time." Decker wiped one hand on his jeans and then held mine with it. "I'm kind of a loner, Mila, so this venture is something I'm not too sure about. The second part of what I have to say is about you."

"I can't wait."

"I can't tell if you're being serious or giving me shit right now."

I smiled. "Then you might want to rethink working for an intelligence company."

"Got it. Giving me shit. Moving along."

"Wow, you're better at it than I thought." I leaned forward and kissed his cheek.

"I've never told anyone half of what I just told you in the last ten minutes. You asked me if I thought you'd be upset. The truth is, that never occurred to me. I'm used to making a decision and then acting on it. What I'm not used to is having to okay it with anyone but the person who hired me. Half the time, I don't even do that."

"And somehow, you get more work."

He shrugged. "I'm good. I'm better than good. I'd say I'm the best, but there's one person who's better than me."

"One? Just one?"

"I know you're bustin' my balls right now, but I'm not lying to you. I really am that good."

"No lack of self-confidence."

He looked down at where our hands were joined. "Not when it comes to work."

"With other things?"

"Truth is, I haven't cared much. I'm a take-me-or-leave-me kinda guy. Don't like me? I really don't give a shit." He turned his body so he was facing me. "You, on the other hand…"

I felt my cheeks flush. How crazy was it that I wanted to be different? That I wanted him to say that he cared about my opinion? "What about me?"

"This Adler guy. I can't tell if I hate him because my instincts are telling me there's something to hate, or if I hate him because I can't stand the thought of him with you."

"He isn't with me, Decker. We're friends. I'm not even sure about that anymore."

"Well, I'm not sure about anything between you and him, and that isn't like me."

"I feel like there's more you haven't said."

Decker put his arm around my shoulders. "There's a lot more, but I don't think we need to get into it tonight."

"You said that you asked these guys to look into Adler's background."

"That's right."

"Are they also looking into what happened to my sister?"

"Yeah. They are."

I looked out at the creek, knowing there were more questions I should ask, but like Decker, I wasn't sure I wanted to get into it tonight.

"I can't make sense of how I feel about you, Mila, and that's not like me either. All I know is that I can't stand the thought of anything bad happening to you. I can't stand the thought of you getting on a plane and going back to Boston, and I sure as hell can't stand the thought of Adler Livingston having a key to your apartment."

"I'm really glad you brought me here, Decker. To the cabin, I mean. It's like the rest of the world doesn't exist for now."

"We can stay on here as long as you'd like."

I laughed. "We have enough food to stay a week."

"Do you still want to go to the cemetery tomorrow?"

Did I? As long as we could stay at this cabin in the woods, sit by the creek, take walks, hold hands, and talk, that was enough doing for now.

"Hungry?" he asked.

"Starving."

14

Decker

I couldn't say for sure if I felt better or worse after telling Mila everything I had. She sure as shit didn't need any more baggage dumped on her shoulders, but she also deserved the truth. If I'd told her in any way other than how I did, I wouldn't have felt like I was being completely honest.

"You didn't say whether you've made a decision about working for the company you mentioned."

I put my hands on the edge of the kitchen counter and rolled my shoulders. "I've decided to accept their offer."

Mila set the food she was getting out of the refrigerator down and came to stand next to me.

"You don't sound happy about it."

It wasn't unhappy I was feeling; it was irritation. Rile had made a bargain with me. The Invincible team would help as long as I agreed to come on board. I wasn't about to tell Mila that, though. It would make her feel as though I'd done something I didn't want to, because of her. If I lied, though, there was a good chance she'd pick up on it.

"The truth is, I'd decided to accept their offer. I just hadn't planned on telling them as soon as I did."

"But you did it for me."

"I did it now, in part, because of you, but as I said, I had already decided to take their offer."

"What does it mean in terms of the ranch?"

"I don't expect things to change too drastically. I've worked with each of these men before, so they're accustomed to when I can take on assignments and when I can't."

She walked back to where she'd set the food, but I sensed she'd left something unsaid. That she was biting her bottom lip told me it was something she was concerned about. I walked over and rested my hand on the small of her back. "What's bothering you?"

She took a breath as if she was going to speak, but then closed her mouth.

"Mila…"

"It's nothing."

I put my hands on her shoulders and turned her to face me. "I told you a whole helluva lot more than I'm used to telling anyone. Please tell me what's on your mind."

"There isn't anything on my mind."

I moved my arms to encircle her waist and looked into her eyes. "I can wait. I'm a very patient man."

She laughed. "I doubt that's true, and the reason I don't want to answer you is because it was silly."

I raised a brow but, otherwise, didn't move.

"Okay." She let out a deep breath. "I was wondering if you'd have to be away a lot."

"From?"

"The ranch. The States."

"And you?"

Her cheeks flamed, and she tried to wiggle out of my grasp.

"Look at me," I said when she looked everywhere but. When she did, I cupped her face with my palm. "Believe me, I've already taken that into consideration."

She smiled, but I knew she didn't buy it.

I brushed her lips with mine. "You don't think I know how crazy that sounds?"

"I live in Boston..."

My first reaction was to tell her she used to live there, but things were already moving so quickly between us that I stopped myself from taking it a step too far and telling her I never wanted her to leave. The fact that she'd taken into consideration that we might not see each other, made me happier than I could say.

We made dinner, dancing around each other in the small kitchen as though we'd done it many times before. Being with her was easier than anyone I'd spent time with before, except for Quint, who had been my best friend for years. And that was entirely different.

I was attracted to Mila, but I wasn't nervous around her, and most of the time, she wasn't anxious with me either. She'd mentioned that she didn't like to be touched, and yet I never saw signs that she was bothered when I put my hands on her—and I did it every chance I got.

After we finished eating and had cleaned up, I led Mila over to the sofa that sat in front of the big stone fireplace. It was too hot to build a fire, but it was the only place where we could sit inside where I could draw her into my arms.

"Come here," I said, nestling her closer to me. She settled in and rested her head on my chest. "I want to ask you about something."

"Okay," I heard her murmur.

"You don't have to answer anything I ask if you don't want to."

"Go ahead."

"You told me that you don't like to be touched."

She tensed and tried to sit up, but I'd kept my arm around her shoulders for a reason. I kissed the top of her head.

"I touch you a lot, yet you don't seem bothered by it. In fact, I think you kind of like it."

I could feel her tense muscles relax, and if I could see her reflection, I'd guess she was smiling.

"I do like it, and to be honest, initially it surprised me too. Now it just feels natural."

Resting my head against hers, my mouth close to her ear, I drew circles on her shoulder with my fingertips. "Tell me why you don't like it, Mila."

"It isn't something I talk about."

I brought my fingers to her neck and gently kneaded it. "Did someone touch you in a way you didn't want?"

It took a while, but eventually, she nodded.

"Before you moved to Boston?"

She nodded again. "It's one of the reasons I left."

It was all I could do to keep my anger in check. If she sensed it, she'd clam up. "Was it someone close to you?"

Mila shook her head. "I'd rather not talk about it."

"If I ever do anything to make you uncomfortable, I want you to tell me."

She didn't answer with words, but she snuggled closer to me, and that told me everything I needed to know. Mila trusted me, and I wouldn't do anything to make her regret doing so.

It wasn't long before her breathing evened out and I knew she was asleep. It was another example of her trust in me. I closed my eyes, not wanting to wake her. When I did, she'd go into one room to sleep and me another; I wasn't ready to let go yet.

It was quiet out in the woods. I could hear the creek bubbling out front and the sounds of wildlife in the distance, but when I heard something that sounded like footsteps, my eyes opened wide.

I gently eased myself out from under Mila, propped her up with a pillow, and crept over to the closest window. The only light inside the cabin was a single candle burning, so I doubted anyone could see much. They'd see my shadow in front of the window, though, so I stayed off to the side, drew my gun from my calf holster, and looked in the direction I'd heard the noise. It wasn't long until I heard the sound of a vehicle's engine off in the distance. I crept to the door and eased outside, staying close to the cabin as I looked around. Without much light from the moon, I couldn't see if there were footprints, but I'd check all around the structure in the morning.

I went back inside, where Mila was still asleep on the sofa. While my plan had been to sleep in separate rooms, there was no way I'd let her out of my sight now. I scooped her into my arms and carried her into the first bedroom I came to. Unlike the others that had smaller beds, this one had a king-size mattress.

She stirred when I eased her body onto the bed.

"Decker?"

"Shh. Go back to sleep."

I lay next to her, only allowing myself to doze on and off.

The sun had been up for at least a couple of hours before Mila woke up.

"Hey," I said when she looked up at me.

"Hi." She removed herself from my grasp, sat up, and looked around the room. "I don't remember coming in here last night."

"You were pretty out of it."

"You slept here?"

"Yep. Just like this." I looked down at my fully clothed body.

"I'm sorry."

"For what? Being exhausted? Don't be."

She got out of bed; I watched as she looked at her phone and powered it back on. When she padded to the restroom, I got up too and straightened the bedclothes. Maybe she'd want to go back to sleep. If so, it would give me time to go out and look around for evidence of anyone being on the property the night before.

Remembering that she'd wanted some yesterday morning, I went into the kitchen to make a pot of coffee. As I waited for it to brew, I peered out the same window I'd stood near the night before. I couldn't see anything from this vantage point, but I'd get out there as soon as I could to take a better look.

"What are you looking at?" Mila asked.

"Nothing. Just waiting for the coffee," I answered without turning to look at her.

"If it's okay, I'd like to take a shower."

"Of course it's okay," I told her, trying to strike the image of her naked body under the streaming water. As soon as she was finished, I'd take a shower too, but mine would be an ice-cold one.

When I heard the bathroom door close, followed by water running, I went outside.

Texas was pretty damn dry this time of year, but next to the creek and under the trees, there was enough humidity that if someone had been walking around last night, they might've left footprints.

I slowly walked toward where I thought I heard the vehicle's engine, shining the light from my phone ahead of me. I could see fine, but the added illumination might make it easier to spot indentations in the ground. About ten yards into the woods, something caught my eye. A twig had snapped and, from it, hung a very small piece of fabric. I looked around that particular area and saw what I'd been looking for—footprints. There was only one set, and from the look of them, I'd say the person who left them wore a size twelve, or bigger, shoe.

I heard another noise and turned to find Mila standing on the front porch of the cabin, watching me with a cup of coffee in her hand.

"What are you doing?" she asked when I walked closer.

"Thought I heard something last night."

"And?"

"There are tracks in the woods, but it's hard to say how old they are."

Mila shuddered and then brought the cup to her lips.

I sat down on the steps, and she joined me.

"Do you think someone was here?"

"I'm not certain."

"But?"

"I know I told you that we could stay here another night or two, but I'd feel more comfortable if we went back to the ranch."

"Okay," she murmured, taking another sip of coffee and then looking around. "I really like it here. I hope I can come back someday."

"I hope so too."

She set her coffee cup down next to her. "When will we leave?"

"I'll take a shower and then pack up the food."

Mila's cheeks flushed before she turned away. I put my fingers on the side of her face and turned her head back toward me.

"What are you thinking, beautiful?"

She shrugged. "I should've asked you to join me. That wasn't very polite on my part."

The look on her face set every one of my nerve endings on fire. I grasped the back of her neck and held her as I captured her mouth in a kiss. When her mouth opened to mine, I deepened it. When she moved closer to me, I lifted her onto my lap. I couldn't kiss her hard enough to quell the urgent need I felt coursing through my veins. She wrapped her arms around me and crushed her breasts into my chest.

I released her lips and kissed down her neck while, at the same time, unfastening the buttons on her blouse. When I felt her tense, I stopped. I moved my hand to her waist and brought my lips back to hers.

"There's no rush, Mila. We'll take this as slow as you need to."

"I'm sorry."

I pulled back and looked into her eyes. "Don't ever apologize for putting on the brakes when you don't feel comfortable. I meant what I said. There's no hurry. As far as I'm concerned, we have all the time in the world to get to know each other. Intimacy, done right, is more than a physical attraction. It's what's in here," I pointed to her head, then to her heart, "and what's in here."

"But I'm the one who…"

"We were both flirting, and there's nothing wrong with that. Neither of us can deny our attraction, but that doesn't mean we're ready to act on our desire."

I brought my lips to hers again and kissed her as deeply as I had before. I wanted her to understand that her pulling back hadn't changed how I felt. I still wanted her, loved the feeling of pressing my lips to her soft mouth, and that was enough for now.

15

Mila

When Deck got up and went inside after being so sweet to reassure me, I wanted to cry in frustration.

It had been almost nine years since one stupid night changed my life. Nine years in which the idea of a man touching my body, shut me down. Nine years that I spent wondering if I'd ever be ready to let go of the fear, the memories, the anxiety that sent me into near panic whenever a man got too close.

I tried counseling, which helped some, and had visited a Sexual Abuse Support Group the therapist recommended. I attended one meeting and never returned.

The other people in the group spoke of horrifying experiences, far worse than what had happened to me. Some talked about how they'd told a person of trust, who didn't believe them or looked the other way.

I hadn't been able to bring myself to talk about what happened to me that night, or how the person I should've been able to trust had saved me only to turn around and betray me.

Had I been harmed mentally and emotionally? Yes. Physically? Not nearly as bad as most of the other people in the group—at least the ones who had shared their stories that day.

I wondered now if I should've tried harder to do the work the therapist had recommended. Worse, whenever I thought about that night, I wondered if I'd made the right decision when I agreed not to report it. But what choice had I had?

I picked up my cup, went inside to get more coffee, and heard my phone's ringtone from the bedroom. By the time I got to it, it had gone silent. I didn't need to look at the screen to know it had been Adler, or listen to the message he left to know why he called.

Why had he come back to Texas? When he'd left for Boston, his attitude had reeked ambivalence. He seemed angry that I refused to fly back with him, but not at all concerned as to why.

When he'd called yesterday, his pleas for me to call him back seemed frantic. Again, why? What had happened between the time he left me standing in front of the sheriff's office and the next morning? I couldn't come up with an explanation that made any sense.

I heard the bathroom door open, and turned to meet Decker's gaze.

"Adler?" he asked, looking at the phone in my hand.

"I missed his call."

Decker nodded and walked into the bedroom. "I've given this some thought."

"Okay…"

"I want to invite him to stay at the ranch."

I was stunned. "Why?"

"It'll give me the opportunity to get a read on him. Not to mention that, in order to do so, he'll need to be scanned into the ranch's security systems. If Rile and the boys haven't found anything on him yet, that'll speed things up."

"If there's anything to find," I added. Was Adler really one of the bad guys? Part of me didn't want to believe it even though another part of me was beginning to believe he was.

"That's right," he responded, albeit half-heartedly. "There's another possibility. He may not want to expose himself to a background check. If that's the case, he'll backpedal. And then, we'll know there's something he's hiding."

I sat on the end of the bed, and Decker sat next to me. "Talk to me, sweetheart."

"There wasn't anything you said that truly surprised me, other than your suggestion that we invite Ad to stay at the ranch. It all makes sense. I'm just having a hard time understanding what he could possibly have to do with my sister's murder. It wasn't like he could've flown to Texas, shot her, and then returned to Boston. He was at my apartment shortly after I got home from work, and stayed with me until the next morning."

"Can you repeat that last sentence for me?"

I leaned over and rested my head on Decker's shoulder. "He slept in the chair."

Deck put his arm around me and kissed the side of my face. "You came pretty close to giving me a reason to rip his arms off."

"I never let him touch me, and I never would. When you were in the shower, I thought about how different it is between you and me. I hardly know you, and yet I feel safe with you. I've never been able to let my guard down with Adler. Not just him, any other man." I turned so I could look into his eyes. "I haven't let another man touch me in nine years, Decker."

I watched as the weight of my words settled on him. There was as much relief etched into his furrowed brow as there was concern. He held me close to him but didn't speak. It wasn't until my phone rang again that either of us did.

"What should I do?" I asked.

"Turn it off."

"But—"

"You can return his call as soon as we're back at the ranch."

Before I could ask another question, I heard a different phone buzz, but I had no idea where the sound was coming from.

16

Decker

I pulled the phone out of my bag. I'd left it on, anxious to hear back from Rile.

"Hello, my friend," the man said, beginning our conversation the way I was growing accustomed to.

"Rile."

"When do you intend to return to Austin?"

"We're leaving for the ranch in a few minutes. Where are you?"

"Our plane was diverted to DFW. We should arrive shortly after you."

"I found evidence that someone paid us a visit last night."

"As your email stated."

That wasn't accurate. My email stated that I suspected someone had been outside the cabin the night before; I hadn't yet confirmed that fact when I sent it.

"I'll be in touch." I ended the call rather than point out the inaccuracy in Rile's statement.

When I went back to look for Mila, I found her gazing out the window. Like yesterday when we were having breakfast, she looked like an angel with the way the sun's rays came in through the window. I stood and stared, not wanting the moment to end. When she turned and smiled, it only intensified the feeling.

"That was Cortez DeLéon. He, Keon Edgemon, and Miles Stone will be meeting us at the ranch this afternoon."

"Your partners."

It would take me some time to get used to thinking of them in that way, but yes, that's who they were.

"Once we're there, I'll ask you to contact Adler and invite him there as well."

"I don't know what I'll say."

"We have a three-hour drive to figure it out."

Having a plan to deal with Livingston, along with knowing I'd have backup from Rile, Edge, and Grinder, left me feeling less anxious than I'd been last night or even this morning.

My gut told him two things. First, Adler was no friend to Mila. He had an agenda. Second, I would be willing to wager that he'd been the one snooping around the cabin the night before. That was the reason I'd asked Mila to turn off her phone. If Adler, or anyone else, had found us at the cabin, that meant someone was tracking her.

Like every other time we'd driven any distance, Mila was asleep not long after we got on the road. Also like every time we'd spent time in my truck, I stole every glance I could at the beautiful woman sitting beside me.

She'd spoken frankly when she told me that she hadn't allowed another man to touch her in nine years. However, I found it troubling that I hadn't found any record of an assault. Whatever had happened was significant enough that it still impacted her in a profound way. The natural assumption was that she had been sexually assaulted. If it had happened nine years ago, she would've been seventeen years old. While some juvenile records were sealed to protect the privacy of the victim, the intelligence networks that the ranch's security system was tied into would've had a record if she'd had as much as a hangnail.

The other thing nagging at me was her lack of a relationship with Judd. She'd made no mention of contacting her father with news of her sister's death, nor had she asked if Mac had contacted him. The only thing she'd said about him was that some people weren't cut out to be parents. I made a mental note to pull a full report on Judd Knight. In my gut, I didn't believe Judd had been the one to assault Mila, but something didn't add up about her relationship with him.

She shifted her body against the seat. I looked over and thought back to our earlier conversation. "I hardly know you, yet I feel safe with you," she'd said. I didn't say it, but ever since the first time I saw her, I'd felt an overpowering need to protect her.

"Decker?"

"Yes, sweetheart?" I smiled.

"Does it bother you that I always fall asleep?"

I grasped her hand, rubbing the back of it with my thumb. "There are occasions that I imagine it would bother me very much. While I'm driving isn't one of them."

Her cheeks turned pink, and she shifted again, this time crossing her feet in front of her. I released her hand and rested mine on her leg.

Her muscles flexed as she squeezed her thighs together, sending a current of need from my hand straight to my cock.

"You can't look at me like that, baby," I said, hating that I had to tear my eyes away from her to watch the road.

"I can't help it."

I groaned. "God, Mila. You're killing me."

"I'm sorry." She spoke the words, but the look on her face said she wasn't the least bit apologetic.

"Do you know how much I want to kiss you right now?"

Her lower lip stuck out just slightly when she nodded and it did me in. I couldn't wait another minute not just to kiss her, but to hold her in my arms, to feel her skin against mine.

I turned the truck off the highway and onto a road that was familiar to me. I parked under a tree and unfastened her seatbelt at the same time as mine. I leaned across the console, my hand on her nape, and pulled her to me. "I'm going to kiss you, Mila, and I'm not going to be gentle about it."

She didn't hesitate. The moment the last word left my mouth, she kissed me. I wanted to hold her, touch her, feel her naked skin, but I kept myself from doing anything more than wind my tongue around hers. I am an aggressor by nature; that's who I am. I couldn't be that way with Mila, though. I had to let her take the lead, let me know what she was comfortable with and how far she was ready to take things between us.

When I pulled back to look at her, something else caught my eye. We were out in the middle of fucking nowhere, but not far from where I'd parked, I could see another vehicle. We had a goddamn tail, and I hadn't noticed.

"Fasten your seatbelt," I said, keeping my eyes on the dark SUV I could see from the passenger-side mirror.

"What's happening?"

"We have company, but don't worry, they won't be with us long."

I threw the truck into gear and put the gas pedal to the floor. Instead of speeding off in the opposite direction, I spun around and drove straight at the other vehicle. Whoever it was—and I intended to find out—would have no time to even get the SUV started, let alone try to escape the oncoming vehicle.

"Keep your seatbelt on, but get down as low as you can," I told Mila.

Gun drawn, I pulled up alongside the other vehicle and fired twice, hitting both tires on the driver's side before I continued back onto the highway.

Part of me had hoped the man behind the wheel was Adler Livingston. It wasn't, which is why I hadn't fired at the driver instead of the tires.

I got off at the next exit and drove down the side roads of the small town until I was certain no one else was following us. I pulled over and held my hand out to Mila, wishing I could still her trembling.

"Did you see who it was?"

"It wasn't Adler." I kept one hand on hers and pulled my phone out with the other. I punched in the license plate number and a description of the vehicle and sent it to Mac before calling him.

"Who do you know in Grover?"

"Allen Bach is the sheriff."

"Have him get whoever is available to State Road 114, about a quarter mile from the highway. Suspected link to Sybil Knight's murder. Vehicle is disabled."

"What did you do?"

"Shot two of the tires."

"Good job."

I ended the call to Mac. The next call I placed was to Rile.

"What's your twenty?" I asked before Rile had the chance to say anything.

"Entering Highway 35."

"I'll send you coordinates in a few minutes. We need an escort."

I set the phone down on the dash. Mila looked at the one sitting on the console. "You have two?"

"Personal and business."

"Which number do I have?"

I picked up the secure line and sent Mila a text. "Both."

Once we got to Waco, I drove to the same restaurant we'd gone to for breakfast on our way to Bluebell Creek.

"Is this okay with you?" I asked when I pulled into the parking lot and sent the text to Rile.

"It's fine," she said, but her cheeks were flushed, perhaps remembering her embarrassment over the declined credit card.

"Would you rather go over there?" I asked, pointing to another diner.

"If you wouldn't mind."

I crossed the road and parked in the lot.

"Wait," Mila said before I got my door all the way open.

"What?" Following her line of sight, I saw what had made Mila warn me; Judd Knight was sitting in the front window, looking directly at her.

17

Mila

It had been nine years since I last saw my father. Before that, it had been an equal number. When I first noticed him sitting near the window, I considered the possibility that he wouldn't recognize me. That hope was quickly squashed. Once his eyes met mine, they remained locked on my face.

His expression was impossible to read. I saw no sign of recognition, no smile, not really a frown—just a steady gaze in my direction.

"What do you want to do?"

I tore my gaze from my father and looked at Decker. "I don't know."

"It's evident you and Judd are estranged."

"That's one way to put it," I mumbled, not necessarily meaning to say the words out loud.

"Your call, sweetheart. I'm happy to drive away."

Was I strong enough to face the man who betrayed my trust, who'd lost the right to be acknowledged as my parent? It seemed with everything I'd been through in the last few days, I felt empowered—as long as Decker was by my side. It was inexplicable, but it was real.

"Let's go in."

Decker opened his door the rest of the way and came around to my side of the truck. When he opened my door and gave me his hand to help me out, I grasped it. "Don't let go of me," I pleaded.

"Never."

By the time we entered the near-empty diner, my father was walking toward us. I stopped, leaving enough room between us that he couldn't reach out and touch me.

"Hello, Mila," he said as if he'd seen me yesterday. "And, Decker."

As much as I wanted to look at Decker to gauge his expression, I couldn't take my eyes off Judd; if I did, he might step closer, which I couldn't allow.

"Why don't we take a seat?" he said, motioning to the booth where he'd been seated.

"I'd prefer a table."

With his hand still holding mine tightly, Decker led us farther into the restaurant. He pulled out a chair for me that faced the door. He took the seat beside me, forcing my father to choose from two that would mean his back was to the entrance.

"You did some damage to one of my vehicles," he said, looking directly at Decker.

"I don't like tails."

"Neither do I."

I studied the exchange between the two men. Decker appeared on high alert, not at all friendly with Judd, which had been my initial concern.

The only read I could get on my father was that he seemed to know he wasn't in control of the situation. It would be interesting to watch him attempt to wrangle it, like he did everything else. My money was on Decker, though.

"I was saddened to hear of your sister's death, Mila."

I opened my mouth to respond and then closed it. Saddened? Interesting word choice. I would think that a parent who lost a child would be devastated, inconsolable. Sad was something an acquaintance might feel, not a father.

"Who told you?"

"The sheriff."

"I'll make arrangements to have her buried in Bluebell Creek next to Mom." Why had I told him that? Did he really care what happened to Sybil's remains? He hadn't even spoken her name.

"Can I get y'all anything?" asked a waitress as she approached our table. "Oh, y'all didn't even get menus. I'll be right back."

I let go of Decker's hand and pushed back my chair. "That won't be necessary. We're leaving."

Decker stood and put his hand on the small of my back as we exited the diner. When he held the door open for me, I froze. Three men were getting out of an SUV parked next to Deck's truck.

"They're with us," he whispered into my ear, but then continued walking toward the truck as though he didn't know them.

We were on the highway before Decker spoke. "I won't feel comfortable until I get you back to the ranch, even with an escort."

I nodded when he looked over at me.

"Is there anything you'd like to talk about?"

"Do you mean Judd?"

Decker shrugged. "He's the elephant in the backseat."

I smiled. "You have a knack for putting me at ease, Decker Ashford."

He reached over and squeezed my leg right above my knee.

"I don't have a relationship with my father. I haven't for a very long time." Had I ever, if I really thought about it?

"Since your parents' divorce?"

"It felt like he abandoned us. Although, to be honest, we were never close."

"When's the last time you saw him?"

"It's been a long time," I mumbled, looking out of the passenger window and praying he wouldn't ask for details. "How well do you know him? You said before that you'd only met him once or twice."

"I recognized him, but didn't know him well enough for him to recognize me."

"That concerns you."

"It does. I'm also concerned that he had someone following us."

I turned in my seat so I could keep my eyes on him as he drove. His jaw was locked tight on the toothpick that hung from the side of his mouth. Every so often, he'd take one hand off the wheel and flex his fingers.

He turned his head, smiled, and winked. "You're awake."

"I like looking at you, Decker."

He reached over and took my hand in his. "Likewise, baby."

"I wasn't sure I'd ever…"

"Keep talkin'. I'm listenin'."

I laughed. "I don't want to scare you."

"Not much does, Mila."

"I just didn't know if I'd ever want to be with a man. But I do, Decker. I want to be with you."

He lifted my hand to his lips and kissed my palm. "I want that too, at whatever pace you're comfortable with."

I closed my eyes and thought about the way Decker had kissed me before he pulled back and noticed the SUV parked not far from us.

At that moment, I'd wanted him so badly I was ready to crawl across the console and straddle his lap. I'd never known what it felt like to desire someone without control, without reason, even before...

When I thought about Decker's hands on my naked body, there was no fear lurking in the back of my mind, only impatient anticipation.

"Will your friends be staying at the house with you?"

"Colleagues, and absolutely not. The ranch has plenty of other places they can stay."

When I turned my phone back on, I expected to find missed calls and messages from Adler, but there weren't any. Not a single one. I should've felt relief; instead, I was perplexed. Had he given up and returned to Boston? If he had, that would be a good thing, right?

Decker came out of his office and closed the door behind him. I held up my phone. "Nothing."

He didn't look surprised, which I also found perplexing.

"What should I do?"

"Wait and see if you hear from him again." He walked over to the front door and let in the three men I'd seen outside the restaurant.

Decker introduced each one. "Mila, this is Cortez DeLéon, also known as Rile."

Of the four men who stood in front of me, Rile was the oldest. His skin was tan and weathered, and while he was bald, his shortly cropped beard was gray. His right arm was covered in tattoos all the way to his wrist, and he was almost as tall as Decker, but with broader shoulders. Until the other men walked in, I would've questioned whether there was anyone alive in better physical condition than Decker Ashford. Each of them exuded power and strength; being in the same room as them was heady, if not overwhelming.

Rile stepped forward and took my hand. He dipped his head and looked into my eyes. "I'm very sorry for your loss, Miss Knight."

"Thank you," I murmured, looking into hazel eyes that, like Decker's, seemed to be peering straight into my soul.

"This is Keon Edgemon, also known as Edge," Decker said when the youngest of them stepped forward.

Edge's unruly dark hair was closely cropped on the sides but a little wild on top. His deep brown eyes held a twinkle of mischief as he brought my hand to his mouth and kissed the back of it.

"That's enough," growled Decker, taking my arm out of Edge's grasp. "And this is Miles Stone, who we call Grinder."

The last man to approach and shake my hand was the most hesitant of the three. His smile was engaging, but behind it, I saw a haunting hint of pain. "It's nice to meet you," he said. "I am also sorry for your loss." There was an edge in his words that spoke of hurt. I found myself wanting to put my arms around him and hug away the sadness in his eyes that mirrored my own.

Grinder took a step back, and the three men turned to Decker, who invited them to take a seat.

I turned to him too, and when I took a step toward the bedroom, he held out his hand. "The conversation we're about to have involves you, sweetheart."

I nodded and came to sit by his side.

Rile sat forward in his chair and took a deep breath. "Your friend from Boston, Adler. What do you know of his background?"

"Not much, to be honest."

"Let's begin with what you do know."

18

Decker

I watched Rile as he walked Mila through what he already knew and what he wanted to know from her perspective. Part of me wished he'd shared the report he obviously had on Adler Livingston, but the other part was fascinated by Rile's technique. As long as the man didn't cross a line that would unfairly put Mila on the defensive, I'd sit back, watch, and listen.

"What about his parents? Have you met them?"

"I have not."

"Do you know how Marshall Livingston accumulated his wealth?"

When I saw Mila flinch, I moved closer and took her hand in mine. The color drained from her face.

"Gentlemen," I heard Rile say, motioning to Edge and Grinder, who both stood and left the room.

"What just happened?" I asked, keeping my voice soft and even.

"Adler's father's name is Marshall?"

"That's right."

Mila wrapped both arms around her stomach. "Can I have some water please?"

I walked to the kitchen, never taking my eyes off of her. I held the glass out for her, and after taking a sip, she handed it back.

Mila stood and walked over to the bookshelves that lined one wall of the living room. She studied the books in them, running her fingers across the spines.

"I met you once before," she said.

"I remember." It was more than that, though. I recalled every detail of that particular day. It was shortly after I'd been taken out of one foster home and placed into another that was on the outskirts of Austin.

The area was predominantly affluent, but my foster parents were from the poor side of town. It was the family that came before my last foster experience—the one that took me to Hays High School where I met Quint Alexander and the trajectory of my life had changed so dramatically.

I'd been thirteen at the time, and the school I attended was so small that elementary and junior high was in the same building.

In my first few days there, I operated in a constant state of anger. Every brush of an arm as I walked through the crowded hallways, put me on edge. As I looked out at the masses of people, I saw every stranger I passed as a potential threat. All I'd known up to that point in my life was that I could trust no one.

The day I first saw her, Mila had been walking toward me, clutching her books to her chest. Three guys that looked close to my age, walked behind her, pushing into her with their bodies as they taunted her. Her face, that day, looked much like it did now.

I hadn't known her name then, but I recognized the fear in her eyes. I'd gotten between her and the three guys.

"Leave her the fuck alone," I remembered seething. I was twice their size and wasn't surprised that they turned and hurried away.

I hadn't seen the girl again who had murmured her thanks and scurried away from me like the guys had. That I was an intimidating fucker wasn't lost on me then or now.

I'd only lived with that foster family another four months, and in that time, I'd looked for her every day.

I hadn't seen her again until I looked into her eyes as she approached me the day I picked her and the asshole Adler up at the airport. I'd immediately recognized the girl I'd seen only one other time in my life yet had never forgotten.

I looked over at her, and she was studying me instead of the books.

"I remember every detail," I told her.

"I asked around that day, and no one knew your name," she said. "My mom worked in the office and looked it up. I think that's why I felt so comfortable around you from the moment I met you. Because it wasn't the first time I met you."

I walked over to where she stood and took her hands in mine. "What set you off before, Mila?"

"Marshall."

"What about him?"

"The man who attacked me. His name was Marshall."

Every alarm, every red flag, every instinct began screaming at me. If Mila weren't standing in front of me with her hands in mine, I would've raced into the office to run a full report on Marshall Livingston.

"Decker?" I heard Rile say.

"Go ahead," Mila told me.

Rile motioned me into the office. The report I would've asked him to start compiling was waiting for me on the desk.

"Give me the short version."

"There's a connection between Judd Knight and Marshall Livingston."

"What?"

"Business adversaries."

I nodded.

"If there's nothing else you need tonight, we'll leave you alone."

"The main house is accessible," I said, turning to Edge. "You know how the system works."

Edge nodded.

Grinder motioned his head in the direction of the living room, and I turned to see Mila walking toward the kitchen. "Take care of her," he said before following Rile and Edge out of the house. "Let us take care of everything else."

"What can I get you?" I asked once the men had left.

"What are you having?" Her eyes never met mine; they darted around, not focusing on anything in particular.

"Mila?"

"Yes?"

I walked over and took her hands in mine. "Mila," I repeated. Finally, she looked into my eyes. "Come with me." I led her over to the sofa and pulled her close to me when we sat down. "Tell me what happened that night."

She shook her head. "It was a long time ago."

"Who have you talked to about it?"

"No one."

19

Mila

No one. That's who I'd told. Absolutely no one. Other than my therapist, but I didn't even tell her the whole story, because my father told me not to.

"Let me handle this, Mila," he'd said after he pulled *Marshall* away from me and slammed him into the wall. I hadn't known his name when he ripped my blouse, scattering the buttons on the floor. I hadn't seen his face when he put his hand on me, tore my bra, and grabbed my breast so hard that I'd had bruises that lingered for days.

It wasn't until my father lunged at the man in the ski mask and called him by name, that I realized what happened wasn't a random act of violence. It wasn't me being in the wrong place at the wrong time. The man who attacked me had planned it.

But how? How had he known I would visit my father that night for the first time in ten years? How had my attacker known I'd beg the man who had abandoned my sister, our mother, and me to please help me pay for college, only to walk back out into the dark night with nothing?

I looked into Decker's green eyes and saw the kindness I always found in them. He said I could trust him, and I knew I could.

"It happened when I was seventeen…"

I told Decker about calling my father and asking if I could meet with him, and him insisting I come after business hours. "It wasn't long after my mother passed away. Maybe a week. I planned to ask him to help me pay for college."

I'd driven into Austin and parked in the lot he'd told me to; it had been empty save for one other vehicle.

"I was anxious the whole way into the city that night, as though I knew something bad was going to happen. I remember thinking that it was because I expected my father to turn me down."

"Did he?"

I nodded. "He said that my mother should have left me more than enough money to go to college."

"Did she?"

"If I had gone to a local college, maybe. But I wanted Sybil to be able to use that money so she could go to college too."

"What happened next?"

"I was waiting…"

Decker brushed away my tears. "Take your time, sweetheart. If this is too much, we can do it tomorrow."

"No. I want to tell you now, Decker." I rested my head on his chest, and he tightened his hold on me.

I sat up and began again. "I was waiting for the elevator, but it seemed like it was stuck on another floor. It didn't move. I was embarrassed that I was crying, and didn't want my father to come out of his office and find me. After waiting for another few minutes, I decided to take the stairs."

"Is that where it happened?"

I nodded. "Between the second and third floors. It all happened so fast; the man came out of nowhere. He slammed me up against the wall and told me not to scream. He covered my mouth with one hand while he ripped my blouse with the other."

"Were you able to see his face?"

"No. He was wearing a ski mask."

"Go on when you're ready, sweetheart."

"He pulled off my bra and grabbed me. I tried to bite his hand that covered my mouth, and he backhanded me. He hit me so hard I thought I was going to lose consciousness. I don't know, maybe I did. The next thing I knew, my father grabbed the guy and threw him up against the wall like he'd done to me."

Decker pulled me closer to him.

"My father yelled for me to go back up to his office and wait for him there."

"Did he tell you to call the police?"

"He told me not to."

"What do you mean?"

"He told me to go upstairs and wait. He screamed at me not to do anything until he got up there."

"And you followed his instructions?"

I nodded again.

"You said his name was Marshall."

"When my father pulled him off of me, he screamed, *'You're a sick fuck, Marshall.'*" There was more I'd heard, but I'd never been able to make sense of it. I shuddered and shook my head.

"How long was it before your father came back to his office?" Decker asked.

"I'm not sure. Maybe fifteen minutes."

"When he got there, he didn't call the police?"

"No. He made me promise not to tell a soul, ever. If I did as he asked, he said he'd pay for me to go to college."

"What happened after that?"

"He gave me a jacket to put on since my blouse was ruined, and then walked me down to my car. Before I was able to get inside, he reminded me of our 'deal.' That's the way he put it, that we had a deal."

I felt sick to my stomach.

"When was the next time you talked to your father?"

"This morning."

Decker stroked my hair and soothed me. "That's enough for tonight," he whispered.

Soon, I felt my eyes drifting closed, and I didn't bother to fight it.

When I woke again, the sun was coming in through the window curtains and I was on the bed, fully clothed like I'd been the night before. There was a blanket covering me, but Decker wasn't beside me. There was no clock in the room, so I could only go by how high the sun was in the sky to try to guess the time. I sat up and was straightening my clothes when I heard the door open.

"I thought you might like some coffee," Decker said, walking over to hand me the cup.

"Thank you," I murmured. I took a sip and studied the steaming liquid rather than look over at him when he sat down beside me.

"I know it was wrong," I said.

Decker took the coffee from my hand and set it on the bedside table.

"If you mean any part of what you did or didn't do that night, or in the days, weeks, months, and even years afterward, you didn't do a single thing wrong, Mila. Nothing."

"I thought he killed him, Decker, and I didn't tell anyone."

Decker looked into my eyes. "If it had been me who found you in that stairwell, I would've killed the man assaulting you."

20

Decker

The least surprising detail of everything Mila had told me about the assault was that Judd Knight had handled the aftermath himself. It explained a great deal about her lack of any kind of relationship with the man.

If the "Marshall" who attacked Mila was still alive, and was Adler's father, I couldn't help but wonder why Judd let her live in an apartment building owned by the man—unless he didn't know.

Later this morning, I'd meet with Rile, Edge, and Grinder to fill them in about what I'd learned so we could plan our next steps.

While it was vital to determine whether Marshall Livingston was the man who'd attacked Mila, how that related to Sybil's murder was the bigger mystery. There was a chance it didn't relate at all, although that wasn't what my gut was telling me.

The other two questions puzzling me were where Adler had disappeared to, along with why Judd Knight had someone tail us on our way home from Bluebell Creek. And, was that who had been creeping outside the cabin the night before?

The other thing that lingered in the back of my mind was how long it had been since I'd done any of the ranch work that was accumulating daily.

"I can hear you thinking."

I laughed. "Yeah? That loud, huh?"

Mila stood and held her hand out to me. "You don't have to handle me with kid gloves, you know. Not about this. I'm okay, Decker. I know I just told you that you make me feel safe, but I haven't lived the last nine years of my life in fear."

"I know you haven't." The way she'd dealt with identifying her sister's body, Adler's bullshit, and more than anything else, confronting her father, proved her words true.

"I know I haven't truly dealt with what happened to me. If I had, my reaction to hearing the name *Marshall* wouldn't have been so intense."

"I sense a *but* at the end of your sentence," I said, following her out to the kitchen.

"I've compartmentalized. I keep myself out of situations that make me uncomfortable as best as I can, and I've learned how to protect myself."

"I'm glad to hear that."

"Someone killed my sister, Decker. I need to know who and why. That's the most important thing to me right now."

"Understood, and I agree." Unless they were somehow connected, but it was too early in the investigation for me to verbally theorize. "There are some things I need to take care of this morning."

"Understood," she repeated, giving me a half-smile.

"You alluded to not being the biggest fan of Texas, but I was wondering if you'd be interested in riding out on the ranch with me this morning?"

She appeared to be thinking it over.

"No pressure," I added.

"It's been a long time since I've thrown a leg over, Decker."

"It's like riding a bicycle." I winked.

Mila smiled, fully this time. "But no pressure." She took a deep breath and let it out slowly. "Sure, I'll ride out with you. Why not?"

"We'll stop up at the main house and get you some clothes to ride in. The Invincible guys are there too. The five of us can continue our discussion from last night."

"The Invincible guys? I kind of like that. Although, won't you hire women too?"

I shrugged. "I guess so."

"Then drop the guy part. Just call yourselves the Invincibles."

"You understand that there is no shortage of over-inflated ego amongst these guys, right? Start calling them that, and you won't be able to be in the same room with them."

"You're one of them, Decker."

I smiled. "That's what I'm talking about. You've already busted my balls about my over-inflated sense of self."

"I can't believe I'm saying this out loud, but maybe it isn't so inflated."

I poured her another cup of coffee and one for myself, and then sent a text to Rile, letting him know we were headed to the main house.

"Good morning," said Grinder, who was standing in the kitchen when I walked in with Mila. He motioned to a pot. "Coffee?"

"No, thank you," Mila answered.

"If that's Quint's coffee, I don't recommend anyone have more than a cup. That shit will float a horseshoe."

"I figured that out." When Grinder tilted his cup, it looked as though half of what was in it was milk.

"Good morning, my friend," said Rile, joining us in the kitchen. He walked straight over to Mila and looked into her eyes. "I regret upsetting you last evening."

"It's okay. I was in shock more than upset."

"I know this is difficult for you."

I rolled my eyes. *Damn smarmy Spaniard.* I looked at Mila, who was smiling at me, perhaps thinking the same thing I was. Rile was smooth, no question about that. I was happy to know that Mila saw right through him.

"We're going to ride out this morning. When we get back, the five of us can continue our discussion from last night."

Rile nodded, walked over to the cupboard, and poured himself a cup of coffee, which he proceeded to drink black. I cringed, remembering how bitter that shit was. It figured that Rile didn't seem to think it so.

"Did I hear you say you were riding out this morning?" asked Edge, walking into the room.

"Yep."

"I'll ride along."

I nodded. When he was last at the ranch, Edge rode out every chance he got. At first, I thought having him along would be a pain in the ass, but the Brit held his own and then some. He was an accomplished rider who took to ranch work like he'd been doing it all his life.

"Got a minute?" I asked Rile.

"Of course," he responded.

"Edge, can you show Mila where the tack room is? There should be something of Wren's in there that she can wear."

"Do you want some coffee first?" Grinder asked.

Edge made a face and shook his head. "I don't know how anyone drinks that bloody stuff."

Once the back door closed behind them, I sat down at the kitchen table.

"What more were you able to learn about Marshall Livingston's relationship with Judd Knight?" I asked.

"They were roommates in college. After they graduated, they went into business together. They had a falling out in 2002."

"Around the same time Judd and Nancy divorced."

"That's correct," confirmed Rile.

"Obvious assumption is the two were related," said Grinder.

I agreed.

"I need a twenty on Adler Livingston. The same day he flew back to Boston, he told Mila he was returning to Texas the next morning. He called and told her he'd meet her in Bluebell Creek. That was the last she heard from him."

"On it," said Grinder. "Anything else?"

"Judd Knight. He was the one who put the tail on us yesterday. I want to know why. Somehow this all relates to Mila's sister's murder." I turned to Rile, who was looking at his phone. "What's on your mind?"

"I want to bring Casper in on this."

Grinder raised his head. "Calla?"

Rile nodded.

"Where is she?" Grinder asked.

"Miami."

"Either one of you want to include me in this conversation?" I asked.

"Calla Rey."

"Never heard of her."

Rile raised a brow. "Surprising."

I backed away from the table, stood, and shook my head. I was regretting my decision to partner up with the Invincibles, as Mila had called them. Rile's bullshit already grated on me.

"Grinder will prepare her dossier and have it for you this afternoon."

"Not necessary," I said as I turned to walk out.

"But it is, my friend. Our intention is to ask Casper to join the firm."

"So do it. You don't need my input."

"Has to be unanimous," said Grinder. "We all have to agree."

Great. More fucking administrative bullshit. What had I gotten myself into?

When I got to the barn, I saw Edge was saddling up Sage, the horse I would've chosen for Mila.

"I can do that myself," I heard her say.

"Let her," I said to Edge.

I watched out of the corner of my eye to make sure Edge did as I asked before I went to look for Boon, the barn manager. I found him in the office.

"Hey, Deck," the man said when I walked in.

"Everything running smoothly?"

"Course it is. Ain't much to keep the hands busy this time of year, but you know that better than I do."

King-Alexander was one of the few ranches in the area that kept a large crew employed year-round. Like Z and even Wasp King before him, Quint and I agreed that what we spent in extra wages, saved us money in the long run. The ranch hands were loyal and worked hard. During the busier seasons, we weren't forced to hire people we hadn't yet vetted, which was necessary with our operation.

"Appreciate you handlin' things here at the ranch, Boon."

"It's my job, Deck."

"You started up the Bummer lately?"

That got a smile out of him. Driving the Bummer was a perk of Boon's job. Quint and I built the Frankenstein truck ourselves. We'd pieced it together from parts of countless others. Once it was assembled, I'd found buckets of bright yellow texture paint, and that's what we'd used to paint it. It had four rows of seats, all-wheel drive, was lifted higher than any of our other trucks, and the tires were from an abandoned military vehicle.

While it didn't really resemble any other vehicle in existence, when some asshole from a nearby ranch bought an old Hummer H1, Quint and I decided our monstrosity looked like a damn sad version of the Humvee, the basis for the H1. That's when we'd started calling it the Bummer.

"Took it out just yesterday," said Boon.

I clapped the man on the back before heading out to saddle up my own horse.

Ike was the first in my string, sired by the same stud as Gunsmoke, Quint's Paint. A year younger than Gunsmoke, Ike was a fifteen-hand, five-year-old gelding, and in my opinion, a far superior horse. Quint disagreed, of course, but really it was just another thing we gave each other shit about.

It made me feel like a pussy, but I missed my best friend. I wondered what Quint's take would've been on Rile's proposal. Most likely he would've been in favor of me signing on the dotted line. Quint was always telling me that I shouldn't use the ranch as an excuse not to do the kind of work I loved.

Except I loved both kinds of work equally, especially at King-Alexander. This place was my home and had been for the last eighteen years. Before Z told me I could stay here with them, I'd never known what having a home felt like. From my earliest memory, I'd bounced from place to place, never feeling like I belonged. I couldn't imagine ever leaving.

"Where's Edge?" I asked Mila when I came out and saw her warming Sage up in the arena.

"He said he wanted to check on something in School-house."

"What kind of rider are you, Mila?"

"I've ridden a time or two."

I smiled when she smirked. It was obvious that she was comfortable in her seat, and while Sage was a sound and manageable mount, like most horses, she responded best to a confident hand.

"Ready?" I asked, opening the gate.

"Whenever you are," she answered, walking Sage out of the arena.

I closed the gate, mounted Ike, and gave him a quick nudge. We moved together easily from a walk to a trot and then into a canter. I let Mila take the lead at edging Sage into a gallop. Once she had, I rode ahead of her, leading her to the upper pasture known as Schoolhouse, where Edge told her he'd be.

She had her blonde hair pulled back, but her ponytail was long enough that it waved in the breeze behind her.

The smile on her face couldn't have been more natural; she obviously loved being on horseback as much as I did. To me, there was no freer feeling in the world. Riding out gave me the space and time I needed to think. I'd needed to get out here more than I realized.

"You look like you're enjoying yourself," I said when we slowed to go over a crest.

"Like I said, it's been a long time. God, I can't even remember the last time I was on horseback."

"It's my therapy. If I haven't had time to ride, pretty much everyone at the ranch knows it." I laughed and then looked up at where Edge was fussing with a section of the fence.

I rode up, dismounted, and tied Ike to a post. I was about to help Mila do the same, but she'd already tied Sage off.

"Looks like somebody got twisted up," Edge said when I got close enough to see what he was doing.

Sure enough, this section of the fence was mangled. I knelt down when something caught my eye. It looked similar to the fabric I'd seen snagged on the broken twig outside the cabin. I pulled out my bandanna and grasped the material with it before rolling it up and putting it in my pocket.

My cell vibrated, and I pulled it out of my other pocket. "Hey, Boon."

"Rile is lookin' for ya."

"Tell him I'll be back in fifteen."

"All three of ya."

"Understood. Send somebody out to Schoolhouse, Boon. We've got some fence to mend. Better yet, I'd prefer you handle it."

"Got it, boss."

21

Mila

It didn't take long for me to feel comfortable, even though it had been years since I rode a horse. When I left Texas nine years ago, I left more than the memories of my attack behind. I left everything—as much as I could anyway.

I donated my riding boots and most of my jeans to a local women's shelter. Anything flannel went to them too, or into the trash. I did my damndest to lose my accent, and when I arrived in Boston, I hit up every thrift store I could find, in search of the kind of clothes I saw my classmates wearing.

Like Adler, I'd been anxious to return to the East Coast shortly after our plane landed. Looking into Decker's eyes at the airport, realizing who he was, finding out my sister's death wasn't an accident, made me want to stay. I couldn't say for how long; I still had a life in Boston to get back to. I needed answers first, though. Starting with, where the hell had Adler disappeared to?

"Everything okay?" Decker asked when we were almost back to the barn.

"Thinking about Adler."

When he growled, I laughed. "Don't tell me you haven't wondered what he's up to."

"I'm hoping that's part of what Rile needs to speak with us about."

When I dismounted, a man was there to take Sage's reins.

"Mila, this is Boon. He's the barn manager."

"It's nice to meet you."

Boon tipped his hat and then removed it. "I was sorry to hear about your sister. I knew your mama."

"Thank you," I murmured, taking Decker's hand when he held it out to me. We walked out of the arena and into the barn.

"Go ahead and change back into your other clothes," he told me. "If we ride out again today, it won't be until much later. It's getting too damn hot for anyone to be out there."

When we rode back in, I'd noticed men checking water supplies in some of the pastures we passed. Instead of on horseback, they'd been on ATVs.

Decker was waiting for me when I came out of the tack room.

"I'll just put these back," I told him, holding up the handful of clothes I'd worn.

"I'll take care of it," said Edge, who I hadn't seen standing nearby.

I was about to argue that I could handle putting the jeans, shirt, socks, and boots back where I'd found them, but when I saw the look on Decker's face, I let it go.

He led me inside to where Rile and Grinder were waiting in what looked like a formal dining room.

"Here you go," Grinder said to Decker, handing him an envelope. He set it on the table and then pulled out the chair next to Rile for me.

"Thank you," I murmured, looking over my shoulder at him. He kissed my cheek and then sat next to me.

Within a couple of minutes, Edge came in and joined them. Once he was seated, Rile leaned forward, resting one arm on the table and looking directly at me.

"We cut our conversation last evening short. My intention is for us to continue at this time."

I nodded. "Okay."

"I asked what you knew about Adler Livingston's parents, and as evidenced by your reaction, you know very little."

"That's right. I never met them." I rolled my shoulders trying to let go of some of the tension that always settled there.

"When is the last time you heard from Adler?"

I looked at Deck and then took out my phone to check. "The day before yesterday."

"I understand that you had an interaction with your father yesterday."

"That's right," I repeated, wishing Decker could just answer so I wouldn't have to talk about it.

Rile looked at Decker, who nodded, and then back at me. "Can you tell me about your conversation?"

"There isn't much to tell. My father interacted with Decker more than with me."

After each answer, Rile nodded. "Before yesterday, when did you last see him."

"Nine years ago."

He leaned in closer. "Are you comfortable talking about what happened the last time you saw him?"

"Comfortable isn't a word I'd use, but I will tell you." I felt Decker's arm across the back of my chair; his fingertips grazed my shoulder.

"I contacted my father and asked to meet with him," I began and continued with everything I'd told Decker the night before, through to the part when my father had walked me to my car after reminding me that I'd agreed not to tell anyone what had happened. While it was easier to tell the story this time than it had been with Decker, having to think so much about that night brought back memories I would prefer be forgotten.

"Can you remember anything else significant that happened that night?" Rile asked.

"Just one thing." I turned to Decker. "I didn't tell you this last night, but when my father yelled for me to leave and wait for him upstairs, I heard something else."

"Go ahead," Decker murmured.

"I heard the man say, 'She looks just like...' That was it. The next thing I heard was what sounded like my father punching him."

"Is there anything else?"

"No, I don't think so."

"Your parents divorced when you were quite young. Is there anything you recall from that period of time?"

"I don't remember much of anything. My father wasn't around very often."

"Your sister was two years younger than you are, is that correct?"

"No, not two. She was fifteen months younger than me." I took a deep breath and leaned back in my chair. Decker had warned me that I would be questioned; it was more difficult than I thought it would be since Rile's questions seemed to jump all over the place. "Wait. There is something I remember."

"Go ahead," murmured Decker.

"My sister needed surgery. Her appendix, I think. It seemed like right after she got out of the hospital, my mama told me we were moving to Bluebell Creek to live with my granddaddy, and that my father wasn't going with us."

When Rile nodded, both Edge and Grinder got up and left the table.

"What's going on?" I asked, looking between him and Decker.

"Research," Decker murmured, and then pushed his chair back. "If there's nothing else you need now, Mila and I are going back to the house."

Rile nodded in the same way he had before Edge and Grinder left the room.

"He's an interesting guy," I said once we were in Decker's truck and pulling away from the main house.

"Bugs the shit outta me, if you want to know the truth."

"It's obvious."

"It is?"

"You spend most of the time snarling when he's talking. Even when he's not."

Decker laughed.

"I guess that's why people call him Rile."

"Good point," said Decker. "Most of the time, I don't pay much attention to the code names these agencies seem to think are necessary."

"Both Edge and Grinder are pretty obvious because of their last names, but I'll admit I was curious about Rile."

"Now you know," Decker snarled, which made me laugh.

"Why are we back here?" I asked when he pulled into the garage.

"Because this morning took more out of you than you think it did. And I'm hungry."

When he came around to my side of the truck and opened my door, I hesitated before getting out. "Why else are we here, Decker?"

He put his hands on my waist and lifted me from the truck, but he didn't set me on my feet. "Couple of reasons," he said, capturing my lips with his. "That's one."

"And the other?"

"I've got some research of my own to do."

Decker slid me down his body and kissed me again once my feet were on the garage floor. "Come on, baby," he said, pulling me toward the door to the house. "After we eat, let's see if we can figure out where ol' Adler disappeared to."

Once inside, I washed my hands and then opened the refrigerator. We'd brought so much food back with us from Bluebell Creek, there was plenty to choose from.

While Decker went into the office, I made a charcuterie board with different kinds of cheeses, raspberries, grapes, chunks of pineapple, and dry salami. I turned the oven to warm, wrapped a baguette in a damp towel, and stuck it in for a few minutes.

"Wow," said Decker when he joined me in the kitchen. "That looks great."

He got out two plates and set them on the counter along with napkins. When I sat in the stool, he kissed me. "Thank you, Mila."

I smiled. "You're welcome, Decker."

"I can't decide what I want more, lunch or to keep doing this." When he kissed me again, I wrapped my arms around his neck.

"This," I murmured, kissing him back.

He cupped my cheek with his hand and looked into my eyes. "I want you to know how brave I think you are, Mila. I know I don't have any right to say this, but I'm proud of you."

"That means a lot to me, Decker."

He picked up a piece of pineapple and took a bite. "I have a question for you," he said after he'd taken a seat.

More questions? I braced myself. "Go ahead."

"How much of this do you want to be involved in?"

"By this, do you mean the work you and your partners are doing?"

Decker put a piece of cheese and salami on a warm slice of bread, took a bite, and then nodded.

"As much as you'll let me be." It might be easier if I'd said I didn't want to be involved in any of it, but Sybil was my sister. I owed it to her to do whatever I could to help figure who killed her and why.

"Are you sure? I warned you that it can get rough."

"I don't have anything else to hide, Decker. I told you my biggest fear, and that's whether or not my father killed the man who attacked me."

"What if we find out he didn't?"

"I'm not sure how to answer you. I haven't ever let myself think about it. I suppose my question then would be, are there others he's done this to?"

"Valid question. And if we find out he did?"

"What would that mean for me from a legal standpoint?"

"That depends on Judd."

"Would you be obligated to report him to...someone?"

Decker pushed his plate to the side and rested his elbows on the counter in front of him. "That's a good way to put it, Mila, and the answer is no. We wouldn't be obligated."

"I don't know whether to feel reassured or concerned."

Decker smiled. "Both."

"So...Adler?"

"I'm having a buddy pull his travel records now. I suspect he's still in Texas, but what he's up to is anyone's guess."

"I could try calling him back."

"You could."

"But?"

"Let's see what my buddy comes up with, and then we'll decide."

"How long will that take?"

Decker refilled his plate. "Long enough for us to finish lunch and then maybe get started on that other stuff we both wanted more of."

22

Decker

"Come with me," I said when Mila finished eating and began clearing our dishes. I held out my hand, and she put hers in it.

"Where are we going?"

"Just in here," I said, leading her over to the sofa. I leaned my back against the arm and settled Mila in between my legs. I ran my hands down her bare arms and rested them on her waist.

"I like having your hands on me," she murmured, trailing her fingertips over them.

"We're going to take this slow, baby. I told you before that I want to know everything I do that makes you uncomfortable. You can tell me, and you can show me. Whichever it is, know that I'm paying attention."

"Can I ask you a question?"

"Always."

"That day in the hallway at school. Why did you make those boys leave me alone?"

I leaned down and kissed her cheek. "It was what I saw in your eyes."

"Fear?"

"Defenselessness."

She snuggled her body deeper into mine. "Do you know how many other kids saw what they were doing and looked the other way?"

"I can guess."

"I never went back to that school."

"I wondered." I'd spent four months looking for her every day, but never saw her again until a few days ago.

"It was a Thursday. By the following Thursday, we'd moved out of our house and had gone to live with my grandfather."

"Where did you live before you moved?"

"Not that far from here. Maybe ten or fifteen miles to the west, right off Old Austin Highway."

"Any idea who lives in that house now?"

"None. I haven't thought about it in years."

I made a mental note to do a property search. Ten or fifteen miles was a big stretch. Either way, it wasn't that far from where I found her sister on the side of the road.

I heard the phone I'd left in the office ringing. Mila started to sit up, but I tightened my hold on her waist.

"Don't you need to get that?"

"I'll call whoever it is back. I'm not ready to let you go yet."

"I have a confession to make."

I smiled. "I like confessions. Especially naughty ones." When she pinched my hand and squirmed against me, I held my breath, willing my cock to ignore her ass grinding against it. I was unsuccessful.

When she spoke again, it was in a whisper. "I've never done this, Decker."

"What haven't you done, baby?"

"This. Any of it." She sighed, turned to her side, and nestled against me. "I worried that I would never be able to let someone touch me the way you do."

I let her words sink in. She said *never,* but she didn't say *again.* Did that mean that before her attack, she'd never been intimate with a man? She was seventeen when it happened, and while that wasn't necessarily the norm these days, it certainly wasn't unheard of for a woman or a man to still be a virgin at that age.

"I wish you'd say something."

I put my fingers on her chin and tilted her head so I could look into her eyes. "Whatever happened or didn't happen before this, doesn't matter to me. The only concern I have is that you feel comfortable with me, want me, want to see where this thing between us goes. I'm in it for the long haul, Mila. I know that might be overwhelming for you, but I believe our souls connected the day our eyes met in the school hallway."

"I feel the same way."

I heard the phone in the office ring again. It stopped and within a minute, started again. Someone was obviously anxious to reach me.

"I better see who's calling." Mila sat up and moved so I could. "We aren't done talking about this, though. Okay?"

She smiled. "Okay."

I hurried into the office but didn't catch the call in time. When I checked the call log, I saw that I'd missed one call from Rile, and two from the man researching Adler Livingston's travel history.

I returned Rile's call first.

"What's up?"

"I've been able to confirm that Judd Knight filed for divorce from his wife before his daughter was even released from the hospital. It would be helpful to review her records."

While my specialty was developing systems to securely protect and safeguard both real property and information, to be able to keep people out, I also needed to be an expert on how they got in. Hacking into something like medical records was child's play compared to the hostile governments and terrorist organizations I'd had to find my way into.

"I'll see what I can find out."

"Casper is on standby. Have you reviewed her dossier?"

"I have more important things on my mind, Rile. If you want to work with her, then do it. You don't need my okay."

I didn't catch whatever the man murmured before ending the call, and I didn't give a shit. If Casper had a role to play in this investigation, so be it. If not, why was Rile wasting time talking about her?

I placed the next call. "Trip, what have you got for me?"

"I know you were looking for travel in the last seventy-two hours, but Adler Livingston is a frequent flier between Boston and DFW. As far as your specific question, he flew in and out of Austin on Tuesday. On Wednesday, he flew in from Boston for a second time. There's no record of him traveling out of Texas yesterday or so far today."

"That takes care of where he is now. Go back to the frequent flier thing you said."

"He's been flying between Logan and DFW on a weekly basis since January. Sometimes flying in and out the same day or within twenty-four hours. Prior to January, it was more infrequent, but it looks like it started up just about a year ago."

"Was he traveling alone or with someone?"

"Alone."

"Always DFW?"

"Mainly, but there were two trips to Austin."

I walked out of the office and into the living room where Mila still sat. "When?"

"One, back in March, and then last week."

"Any other travel?"

"Negative."

"Thanks, Trip. I owe you one."

"You owe me a helluva lot more than one, but don't worry, Decker. Someday, I'll start collecting."

I chuckled and ended the call. I sat down next to Mila. "Did you say Adler traveled on business?"

"Yes, but I don't know anything about it. I'd say that he didn't talk about it, but the truth is, I didn't ask."

I scrubbed my face with my hand and then told Mila everything Trip had told me. She stood and paced, hands on hips.

"Tell me what you're thinking, sweetheart."

"At the moment?"

I nodded.

"I need to pound keys."

I cocked my head.

"Play the piano. It's my stress relief."

"Are you serious?"

She stopped pacing and glared at me. "Are you making fun of me?"

I held up both hands. "Not at all. If you really need to take your frustration out on a piano, I know where you can do it."

"Where?"

"The main house."

"I'm serious about this, Decker. I feel like I'm about to crawl out of my skin."

I stood and walked over to her, taking her hands in mine. "Remember this morning when I told you that riding out is my therapy? I get it. If you need to pound keys or whatever it was you said, I can make that happen. Let's go."

We were partway to the main house when Mila brought up what I'd learned about Adler's recent travels.

"Why was he traveling to Texas?"

"I don't know, but as soon as that sweet tush of yours is planted in front of the piano, I intend to figure it out." I also intended to look into Marshall Livingston's recent travels. And, I still needed to hack into Sybil's medical records to see if there was anything unusual about her surgery or hospital stay.

"Do you remember at which hospital Sybil had her surgery?"

"St. David's Children's Hospital."

I nodded. That wasn't far from the ranch and the only one in the vicinity of Austin, so it made sense that's where her parents would've taken her.

The piano was probably horribly out of tune since no one had played it since Quint's mother died years and years ago. I knew that neither Quint nor his sister ever learned. Mila didn't seem to mind, though, when I escorted her to the library that was toward the back of the house.

"You can close the door," she said when I walked out of the room. I looked over at her before I did, and she was already mesmerized by the instrument.

"If you need me..." I began, but it was pointless; I doubted she heard a word I said. I was partway down the hall when I heard her start to play.

Rile met me when I came into the kitchen. "Where are Edge and Grinder?" I asked.

"Grinder is looking deeper into Judson Knight's association with Marshall Livingston. Edge is on his way to Bluebell Creek."

23

Adler

"I won't be able to get back in there until later tonight. I've already had one neighbor approach me and tell me how sorry she was to hear that Sybil died. She said she knew we were friends, and that she'd pray for me," I told my father.

"It has to be there," he murmured, sounding like he was talking to himself and hadn't heard a word I said.

"I don't understand, Dad. I thought you'd arranged to meet Sybil."

"Judd Knight must've gotten to her first."

"Jesus. Do you think he killed her for it?"

"Fucking focus, Adler! Do you fucking understand what's on the line here? Those documents prove that I was the original applicant on the patents that Knight-hawk's technology is based on. Billions of dollars are at stake."

I let out a deep breath. Was a woman's life worth that? I supposed to my father, it might be. And what kind of man would that make him? "What am I looking for specifically?"

"A flash drive."

24

Decker

"It's kind of like that social media platform that two college students claim to have invented in their dorm room. Twenty years later, only one of them is a billionaire," said Grinder, briefing Rile and me on what he'd learned about Judd Knight and Marshall Livingston. "Knighthawk made its money in inductive wireless technology."

"What is that?" asked Rile.

Grinder looked at me. "You're the techno-wizard."

"It transmits data by way of magnetic induction, which is one of two fields that comprise a radio signal. Electric is the other field. It relies on a coiled transmitter that delivers the magnetic induction signal which is then picked up by another device. So essentially, data, audio, and voice transfer from one device to another. It's more secure than the better-known transmission methodologies."

"What do you use?" Grinder asked.

"You mean, what do we use." said Rile.

"We use Burns Butler's radio technology, which is like ultra-wideband in that it uses a very low energy level for short-range, high-bandwidth communications over a large portion of the radio spectrum. Except with Burns' UWB, the baseline pulses are sent directly from a device's antenna. Its signal strength can infiltrate walls, the ground, and even the human body."

I knew it was unlikely Rile or Grinder had any real idea what I was talking about. It didn't matter; it was why they wanted me to be a partner in their firm in the first place.

While it was Burns who had come up with the original idea, he and I developed the technology together. I was also the one who'd ramped it up, or as Burns liked to say, "added the turbocharger."

When we leased our version of UWB to the US government, it was without my add-ons. That, we kept for ourselves. However, given Burns insisted that my name be on several of the original patents, that deal had made me a very wealthy man.

"Knighthawk is solely owned by Judson Knight. He never took it public," said Grinder. "Which also means he figured out a way to cut Livingston out in the early stages."

"What's it worth?" Rile asked me.

"Initially, millions, but Knighthawk didn't stop there. They took that one piece and applied the technology to nearly every smart device in existence."

"So billions?" asked Grinder.

"At least."

Rile turned to me. "What have you been able to determine about the timing of the divorce filing?"

I told him there was nothing in Sybil Knight's medical history, specifically her surgery, that gave me any clue as to why Judd had filed for divorce. I'd been able to confirm the date of her surgery and the date of the filing, and either Judd had one helluva heartless attorney, which was likely, or something had happened in that four-day period of time that set him off.

"I also reviewed the court documents. It doesn't appear that Judd was ever required to pay alimony or child support." No wonder Mila didn't want anything to do with him. Cheap-ass *sonuvabitch* didn't even want to give her anything so she could go to college.

"The next million-, or billion-, dollar question is whether the Marshall who attacked Mila and Marshall Livingston are one and the same?"

The only thing that made sense to me was that they were two different people. If that was the case, there was a good chance Judd had killed Mila's attacker. Otherwise, nothing he'd done that night made any sense.

My phone vibrated with a message from Edge. *Look who I found*, it said. The next message was a photo of Adler Livingston. Before I could ask any questions, Edge called.

"Talked to a neighbor who said 'that man has been hanging around again.' Her exact next words were, 'he didn't seem that upset, given how good of friends he and that poor girl were.' She's the one that took the photo."

"Where is he now?"

"A couple of cars ahead of me."

"Stay on him, Edge."

Somehow Adler and Marshall Livingston, Judd Knight, and Sybil were connected, and it got her killed. But who'd killed her, and why?

What had made Judd divorce his wife so abruptly right around the time of Sybil's surgery?

My cell rang, and I saw Trip was calling back. I didn't know where or how this guy got his information, but he sure was quick about it.

"What have you got for me?" I asked.

"No commercial travel information on Marshall Livingston. He flies private."

"His own plane?"

"My guess, although it's registered to a shell LLC."

"What kind of data can you get me on it?"

"Manifests are on their way to you now."

"Again, I owe you."

Trip laughed. "I'm getting around to asking you for something."

"What's that?"

"When I'm ready, I'll let you know."

When I checked the time, I was surprised to see that almost an hour had passed since I led Mila to the piano. I could still hear her pounding keys, as she put it.

Knowing she used it for stress relief made me anxious to saddle Ike up again and ride out.

I opened my laptop and perused Marshall Livingston's flight manifests. Unlike Adler, he hadn't spent any time in Texas at all.

I walked down the hallway and eased the library door open. Mila looked up and stopped playing.

"I wanted to let you know that I'm headed to the barn."

She stood.

"You can keep playing."

"No, I need to stop. My shoulders are starting to ache. Plus, if you wouldn't mind, I'd like to go with you."

"Wouldn't mind at all." I sent a message to Boon, letting him know we were on our way out. By the time we got to the barn, both horses were saddled up and ready to go.

"Feel any better?" I asked once we were out on the open range.

"Yes and no. I vacillate."

"That's to be expected." So did I, to be honest. There was something obvious I was overlooking. I just needed to stop trying so hard, and it would come to me. I took a deep breath, trying to figure out the best way to tell Mila that Edge had located Adler, and what the neighbor had said about him and Sybil.

"I've been thinking about Adler—"

"I have something to tell you."

Mila pulled Sage to a stop. "What?"

I dismounted and held onto Ike's reins. Mila did the same. "Let's walk."

"Decker? Whatever it is, just say it."

"Adler and Sybil knew each other. That's where he was, at her house. A neighbor told Edge he'd been there before."

"That's why he was traveling back and forth to Texas? To see my sister?"

"So it seems."

"Why?"

"I don't have the answer to that question yet, but I'm working on it."

When Mila stopped walking, I did too. Her fists were clenched, and she had a look on her face that I hadn't seen before.

"Is my whole fucking life a lie? Is there anyone I can trust? *Jesus.*"

I took one of her hands in mine. "You know the answer to your second question, Mila. You've got me. You can trust me."

"I know. I mean, I think I know. I also thought I could trust Adler. I thought he was my only real friend in Boston. Now I find out that he's a goddamn psycho who's been...what? Was he having sex with her?"

"I can't answer that particular question either."

She huffed and pulled her hand away. I stepped closer and put my arm around her waist.

"Don't doubt me, Mila. I'm the real deal here."

She rested her forehead against my chest. "I know, and I'm sorry I said that. I've never felt so confused."

"Need to pound some more keys?"

"No, but can we ride?"

"Absolutely."

We rode hard for fifteen or twenty minutes. Ike and I could've kept going, Sage too, but Mila was showing signs of fatigue. I had no idea how long it had been since she rode, but it was more difficult than people thought; the rider did as much work as the horse.

Once we slowed to a walk, something from the medical reports I'd read flashed in my mind. *Blood. Sybil had needed a blood transfusion.* God, it was so obvious.

"Do you know your blood type?"

"I don't even want to know why you're asking me that question. But, yeah. A-positive."

"We need to head back."

25

Mila

I hadn't known Decker long, but I doubted there were many occasions when he didn't take care of his own horse after riding out. I heard him apologize to Boon, who in turn, told him that he had plenty of ranch hands standing around with little to do.

Instead of going into the main house, Decker led me over to his truck, opened my door, and gave me a hand climbing in.

"I do better work alone," he said, getting in on the driver's side.

"Do you want me to stay here?"

"No."

I continued to stare at him. His jaw was tight, and I didn't remember him having a toothpick in his mouth when we were riding.

"Sorry," he said, reaching over to hold my hand. "I'd say you don't count, but that isn't the way I mean it at all."

I laughed. "Good."

"It's just that I'm still alone when you're with me." He shook his head and looked away.

"That wasn't much better, Decker."

"I know. Third time's a charm, right?"

"Fourth. Maybe. Gimme what you've got."

"I want you with me every minute of every day, every week, every month, every year—for the rest of my life."

"Wow." I had to catch my breath.

"Too much?"

"Uh...it definitely made up for the first three."

I knew my cheeks were flushed; they felt like they were on fire. I still hadn't fully recovered when Decker pulled into the garage.

"Stay there. Wait for me," he said, noticing me grasping the door handle. When he opened my door and I turned toward him, he put his hands on my waist and lifted me out of the truck. With me still in his arms, he leaned his back up against the truck and pulled my body flush with his.

With one arm still around me, he gripped the side of my face with his other hand. He was close enough to kiss me, but he didn't. He just stared into my eyes. "I know I sound crazy, Mila, but I can't help it. I meant every word I said."

Before I could respond, Decker kissed me harder than he ever had before. God, I wanted this man, and I didn't want to wait.

"Decker, let's go inside."

His eyes searched mine.

"I need to be closer to you."

When his breath caught, I took his hand and led him into the house. I didn't stop when we got to the door to his office, or in the kitchen, or in the living room. I walked straight past the guest room and continued down the hallway until I reached the room I knew was his.

The king-size bed was on a platform and covered by a brightly colored Navajo blanket. The walls were mottled in copper and black, and behind the bed's leather headboard hung a tricolored cowhide. Shelves full of hardcover books flanked each side of the bed, and at the foot, there was a leather-upholstered bench that matched the headboard. Like the rest of the house, everything seemed to be in its place. The bed was even perfectly made.

Decker stood behind me and wrapped one arm around my waist. I turned to face him and then backed out of his grasp.

His eyes flamed as I put my hands on the hem of my shirt, pulled it over my head, and tossed it on the bench. I reached around and unfastened my plain white bra.

"God, Mila," he gasped as I slid it over my arms and tossed it on top of my shirt.

He took a step forward when I unfastened my jeans, and I shook my head. "Don't stop me, Decker. Please."

He dropped his hands to his sides; the look on his face mirrored the need I felt for him. Hooking my thumbs inside my panties, I dropped them with my jeans. Before I could wiggle out of either, I giggled and toed off my boots. So what if my first time stripping for a man wasn't terribly graceful?

He smiled and held out a hand to help keep me steady enough to finish what I'd started.

"Mila—"

I put my fingers to his lips. "Let me do this. It's what I want."

Standing before this man completely naked, I felt no fear. I took his hand and rested his palm on my breast. "Show me how it's supposed to be, Decker."

26

Decker

It was all I could do not to rip my shirt from my body, but if I did that, I'd scare her. It wouldn't be impassioned; she'd see it as the same violent experience she'd suffered in the past.

I drank in every inch of her perfect, naked body, silently thanking God for creating the breathtaking woman standing in front of me.

With a deep breath, I steadied my shaking hands and unfastened the pearl snaps on my shirt one by one. I eased it from my shoulders and froze when Mila put her hands on my bare abs. Her touch seared me, and I groaned.

Like her, I toed off my boots. Before I could unfasten my belt, Mila's hands were on my waist. Her eyes met mine as she pulled the end from the loop and unhooked the tongue from the prong. With my hardness straining against the fly, it wasn't going to be easy for either of us to release the rivets on my jeans.

I stilled her hands. "Before we go any further, I want you to know that I don't have anything on under these."

She pulled air into her lungs and then slowly released it, her anticipation and blatant desire almost driving me insane.

As I eased my jeans over my cock, I heard her take another deep breath when it sprang free, hitting my stomach.

I walked her backward to the bed and lifted her up on the edge. "Open for me, baby," I said, gently easing her legs apart. "I can feel your heat, and I haven't even touched you yet. God, Mila, we're going to combust when I get inside of you."

I cupped her breasts, gently kneading them, flicking her nipples with my thumbs. "Beautiful," I murmured with a rasp when I saw the flare of desire in her eyes.

I took my time running my hands over her body, roaming and appraising, and then bending to take her nipple in my mouth, sucking and teasing until the scent of her arousal overwhelmed me.

Mila tunneled her fingers into my hair, holding me to her breast. "That feels so good," she moaned.

Backing away, I knelt in front of her and skimmed my hands slowly up the inside of her legs, feasting my eyes on the patch of blonde curls at her core.

"So soft," I murmured, allowing my fingertips to drift into her wetness. "God, you're so hot, so tight," I said at the same time she cried out.

I added a second finger, slowly stroking in and out, and Mila fell back against the bed, her hands in her own hair.

Easing her legs farther apart, I lowered my head, sweeping my tongue over her folds before pressing my mouth to her sex. When her hands grasped my hair, trying to move me away, I dove in deeper, my mouth and fingers driving her wild.

"Decker, God," she groaned.

"Hold on tight, baby. This is a ride you'll never forget."

Mila arched her back, and her wet heat clenched around my fingers. Her hips jerked, and her mewling cries were almost enough to bring my release far sooner than I wanted. I covered her trembling body with mine and kissed her neck, her cheeks, her eyelids before finally bringing my lips to hers. My tongue tangled with hers, and she wrapped her legs around me.

"I need more," she groaned, pressing her sex against my hardness.

"Do...not...move," I said, pushing myself up and off of the bed. I walked into the bathroom, opened the middle drawer, and gave a silent prayer of thanks when I spotted the unopened box of condoms I'd forgotten I had. I grabbed a handful and went back into the bedroom.

"Good girl," I said when she'd only moved to writhe.

I lay by her side, running my fingertips over her damp, heated skin. The way this was playing out wasn't anything like I'd envisioned. It was heated, passionate, frenzied. It didn't feel romantic or loving or gentle.

She looked up at me with such longing. "Please," she whispered.

I brought my lips to hers in a soft, slow kiss. "We aren't going to rush this, Mila."

Before I'd hurried, not anymore. There were so many things I wanted to do to her, so many experiences I wanted to share, so many ways I wanted to show her how intimacy between a man and a woman who cared for one another should be. And I did care for her, more than any other woman I'd ever known.

She shuddered as I kissed my way across her body. I ran my tongue under the soft underside of her breast. When I got to her shoulder, I nipped her skin, and then ran my hand down her arms, remembering how I'd longed to reach out and touch her when I met her at the airport. Somewhere in the house, a phone was ringing, and I didn't give a shit. Whoever was calling, whatever they wanted, could wait. Mila, the woman I'd waited for, somehow knew would walk back into my life, was in my arms, and nothing else mattered.

When I shifted my body and rested my head on Mila's tummy, she moved her hand to my leg. "Do you want to touch me, baby?" When she nodded, I took her hand and rested it on my hardness. I let her explore, running her fingers up and down my shaft like I'd done when I took my time running my hands everywhere on her body.

"Show me, Decker," she whispered.

"Like this," I said, wrapping her hand around me and then covering it with my own. I guided her, first soft and slow, and then showed her that she wouldn't hurt me if she held tighter, went faster. I closed my eyes, but only momentarily. On the brink of an orgasm I wasn't ready to have, I stilled her hand.

"Did I hurt you?" she asked with wide eyes.

"No. The opposite. It feels too good."

Mila pushed my hand away and continued stroking me. I closed my eyes, willing my body to wait, and felt the tip of her tongue run the length of me.

"God, Mila," I groaned. "I don't want you to ever stop, but, baby, I need you to stop."

Rather than just moving her hand, I shifted my body so we were side by side. Her eyes were open wide, darting back and forth, studying me.

I leaned forward and captured her mouth with mine, kissing away her insecurities. "The first time, Mila, I want to be inside you. I want you and I to share that, both of us, at the same time. Do you understand?"

"I want that too. I don't want to wait, Decker."

"There's no hurry, sweetheart."

She reached for me again, and I swatted her hand away. She giggled and pushed me back on the bed, resting the upper half of her body on my torso.

I drew circles around her nipple with my fingertip. "Now you see, if we hurried, we would miss out on getting to know each other's bodies." I wrapped my arm around her waist and rolled until she was beneath me. "And I want to know every single inch of this body, Mila."

"You really need to get that," she murmured when the phone rang for the tenth time in thirty minutes.

"I could just turn it off," I said between nibbles on the back of her knee.

"It could be an emergency."

"It's a five-minute ride from the main house here. If it were an emergency, someone would be banging on the door." As if on cue, we heard the sound of someone pounding on a door near the front of the house.

"Dammit," I mumbled, getting up and pulling on my jeans. "Do...not...move," I said like I had earlier. "And if you have to move, do not put any clothes on."

Mila smiled and rolled to her back. I took one more lingering look of the body I doubted I'd ever get enough of.

I'd brought myself back from the brink so many times, my cock ached, but it was worth it. When Mila was naked next to me, I wanted to savor every moment, never rush, never let her leave feeling anything but well sated...and loved.

Halfway down the hallway, I stopped and put my hand on the wall to brace myself. Love? Where in the hell had that come from? I couldn't deny it, though. I wanted to love Mila Knight. Her body, her soul, her mind, everything about her.

Since whoever was pounding on my door seemed relentless, I took a deep breath and went to answer it.

"Sorry," said Grinder, dropping his hand. "Edge needs to speak with you."

"Why me specifically?"

"Because Adler Livingston is headed this way."

"*Jesus,*" I mumbled, walking over to the kitchen counter to pick up my phone. As I waited for Edge to answer, I caught Grinder looking me up and down. *"What?"*

"Sorry, my friend, but no shirt, no shoes, trousers halfway open…appears you had a bloody good reason for ignoring your mobile."

"Damn right, and don't say that. You're starting to sound like Rile."

"What's he saying?" said Edge, answering in the middle of my sentence.

"My friend. 'Hello, my friend,' doesn't that just annoy the hell out of you?"

Both Edge and Grinder laughed.

"What do you want, Edge?"

Grinder leaned forward. "He's pissed because you interrupted him and Mila."

I elbowed him in the gut and turned my back. "Go ahead."

"Livingston is headed south. At first, I thought he might attempt to get onto the ranch, but he's turned off the main road. I've no idea where he's going."

"I have a guess. Call me back when he stops and send me the coordinates."

"Where do you think he's going?" Grinder asked when I ended the call.

"The house Mila and Sybil lived in with their parents before the divorce."

Grinder raised his eyebrows.

I led him outside and closed the door behind us. "I want you to follow up on something else. I need to track down Marshall Livingston's blood type. Also, have the medical examiner confirm that Sybil's was B-negative. Then we'll see if we can find out Judd's."

"Are you suggesting Sybil wasn't Judd's daughter?"

"It would explain the abrupt divorce filing while his kid was recovering from surgery."

"What's Mila's? Does she know?"

"A-positive."

"Is everything okay?" Mila asked when I came back into the bedroom.

"Not really."

"What's wrong?"

"You weren't supposed to get dressed."

"I'm hardly dressed, Decker."

I draped my body across the bed and put my fingers under the hem of her shirt. "No longer naked."

"I just thought...if someone were to come in."

"To the bedroom?"

Mila's cheeks flushed. "I just felt weird."

I kissed the palm of her hand. "It's okay. There's something we need to talk about anyway."

Mila got off the bed and grabbed her jeans. "I'll be right back."

"Wait a minute," I said when I saw the look on her face. "We aren't finished, baby. We're barely getting started."

She looked into my eyes but didn't speak.

"I mean it."

She nodded and left the room, and I felt like the biggest asshole that ever lived. My desire to take things slow had left Mila feeling unwanted, and that was the last thing she should feel.

27

Mila

Tossing the jeans on the bed, I rummaged in my suitcase for a pair of shorts. I was sure I had another clean pair. Given I hadn't planned on being here very long, I didn't pack much. Although I really didn't remember packing at all. Much of the last few days were a blur.

I sat on the end of the bed and put my head in my hands. While Sybil and I never got along, she was still my sister. We'd looked so much alike growing up that people often mistook us for twins, but other than the physical appearance, we'd had almost nothing in common.

If I were asked to describe my sister in three words, the first would be angry. I'd attributed it to my leaving for college shortly after our mother died, but Sybil could've gone to college if she'd wanted to. It wasn't as though our grandfather was in poor health at the time. In fact, he'd only gotten sick a few months before he died.

Sybil had been angry long before that, though. But why? I'd experienced all the same things my younger sister had. Our father had left our mother when we were very young. He went on to make a staggering amount of money, if one could believe the press' accounting. He'd been featured on the cover of several business magazines and even made the list of one hundred wealthiest men in the world. Did it bother me that we didn't share in that wealth? Not really. We'd been happy enough living with our grandfather. It wasn't as though we'd never had enough to eat.

Happy enough. Had we been? While Sybil had been mostly angry all her life, our mother—for as long as I could remember—had been profoundly sad. I didn't remember much before the divorce, so I had no idea if that was the cause of her lifelong depression. I didn't think much about it at the time, but now that I was an adult, I realized the fact that my mother never dated again, as far as I knew, was odd. She'd only been in her early thirties when her marriage ended, yet I never remembered her going on a single date or even expressing an interest in doing so.

Sybil hadn't done much dating either. I'd never met or heard about anyone my sister referred to as a boyfriend. Was that because she and Adler had been secretly seeing each other? The idea of it made me cringe.

I looked up and saw Decker in the doorway, studying me.

"Whatcha' thinkin' about, pretty girl?"

"Honestly? How fucked up my family is."

Decker came and sat beside me. "I'd bet ninety percent of people would say the same thing."

"What about your family, Deck? At the sheriff's office, you said you didn't have anyone. What happened?"

When he scrubbed his face with his hand, I regretted asking.

"The closest thing I have to a family is Quint and Z Alexander."

"You don't have to talk about if it's too personal."

Decker half-smiled. "Baby doll, we spent the last two hours exploring each other's naked bodies, telling you about my family isn't too personal."

"I know, but…"

"My parents both split the scene before I turned seven. They were into drugs, alcohol, God knows what else. After that, I bounced around in the foster system for six years until I met Quint. He invited me to come to the ranch, and I did, every chance I got."

I leaned over and kissed his cheek. "I'm sorry, Decker."

"Don't be," he said. "I have a feeling Z saw that I was being abused, although he never said so directly. One day he just asked me if I wanted to live with them. I've been here ever since." He let out a heavy sigh. "It wasn't just that Z saved me from my fucked-up existence, he's the one who encouraged me to get my degree—paid for it too. And then he hooked me up with Burns Butler, and the rest is history."

"You look up to him."

"Z or Burns? The truth is, I look up to both of them. In a lot of ways, they were both mentors. Still are."

"I haven't had anyone like that in my life. You're lucky, Decker."

He leaned over and kissed my cheek. "Now, I am." He took my hand in his. "There's something we need to talk about. Several things, actually."

"Okay, um, before we do that, is there somewhere I can do laundry?"

"Of course. Come with me."

Decker led me down the hallway to where the washer and dryer were, and then out into the kitchen.

"What did you want to talk to me about?"

He pulled out a stool at the kitchen counter, and I sat. "Adler is in the area. While I don't know exactly where the house is that you lived in before your parents divorced, I have a feeling that might be where he's headed."

I put my head in my hands. What was going on, and what did that old house have to do with it? "I don't understand. Why?"

"Best guess is he's trying to find whatever the people who trashed your sister's house were looking for. Take that a step further. Whatever it is, must have something to do with your sister's murder."

It was logical that someone looking for something would trash my grandfather's place because that's where we lived since we were kids and where Sybil continued to live after he died, but why the house we lived in before that? None of this made sense to me. "What else, Decker?"

He pulled out the stool beside me and sat down. I knew whatever he had to tell me was bad, based on the look on his face.

"I took a look at your sister's medical records. Her blood type is B-negative. It's very rare, and she needed a transfusion before her surgery. I have a suspicion that may have been what ended your parents' marriage. It's possible Sybil wasn't your father's child."

I leaned against the back of the stool. "Are you suggesting my mother had an affair?" Was Decker really suggesting that the only person in my immediate family that I'd believed to be sane, wasn't?

"It's one possibility in terms of why their marriage ended."

"Do you want me to ask my father? Is that what this is about?"

"No. I've asked Grinder to see if he can find his blood type as well as your mother's. It could prove my theory wrong. However, if my suspicions are correct, there may come a time that I or someone else questions your father."

"Is there more?" If so, I might as well hear it all now instead of Decker piecemealing it.

"Two things happened right around the time of your sister's surgery. First is your parents' divorce. The second thing is Judd Knight took over full ownership of Knighthawk. Your father and Adler's father knew each other in college. They were roommates who went on to start the business together."

I studied Decker's face. "That's who you think my mother had an affair with."

"Again, these are theories, Mila. I know you were very young at the time, but do you remember anything that would either support or deny what I'm suggesting?"

"Before you came into the room earlier, I was thinking about my mother and how she was only four years older than I am right now when her marriage ended. To the best of my knowledge, she never dated again. Doesn't that seem odd?"

Decker nodded.

"She was also very strict about Sybil and me dating. Honestly, we were both late bloomers. Speaking for myself, I was so obsessed with my music that I didn't have much time for dating. If I wasn't practicing, at a lesson, or giving a lesson to make extra money, I was doing homework. Sybil, on the other hand, argued with our mother endlessly about her being able to date. The rule was not until we were sixteen."

I startled when there was another knock at the door. Decker stood to answer it, and Rile came in.

"Hello, my friends," he said, addressing both Decker and me.

I smiled when Decker rolled his eyes.

"What can we do for you, Rile?"

"Edge sent a message that he's followed Adler Livingston to what looks like an abandoned dwelling. I've told him to wait for backup to arrive before making any other move."

"Agreed. Is Grinder on his way?"f

"Affirmative. Also, a quick search of the property indicates that it was put into a trust nine years ago. The sole beneficiary of that trust is you, Mila."

"What did you say?" Our old house had been put in a trust for *me*? By whom? It sure as hell wouldn't have been my father.

"The property will not officially become yours until you turn thirty, and while it appears it has been abandoned for some time, property taxes and insurance are current."

"Who owned the house before it was put in the trust?" Decker asked.

"Judson Knight."

Wait a minute. "Not Judson and Nancy Knight?"

"Your mother's name was never on the title."

Whether my mother had an affair or not, the fact that my father had never put her on the title of a house they'd lived in from the start of their marriage, only reinforced how my father operated. I wished my mother, or even my grandfather, was still around so I could ask what in the everliving hell went on back then.

But they weren't. The only person in my family still alive was my father, and I hadn't considered him part of it in a very long time.

"The time has come for us to question Mr. Knight," said Rile, looking between Decker and me.

"Let's wait and see what Adler's next move is first. So far, no one outside of our group knows there's an active investigation. The news outlets haven't picked anything up about the murder, which could mean that whoever is involved, thinks they have time to cover their tracks."

My head snapped up. "Do you think my father killed Sybil?"

"That isn't what my gut is telling me, no," answered Decker.

"Who, then?"

"Given Adler was with you at the time of her death, I'd say either his father or someone he contracted to kill her."

I groaned, put my head in my hands, and pulled my hair. "Why would someone kill Sybil? I just don't understand. Considering how little I knew about my own life, I doubt she knew more."

Rile sat on the stool next to me, which Decker didn't look happy about.

"My understanding is that after your grandfather's death, you paid his medical debts."

"That's right."

"Did it surprise you that he didn't have enough money to do so himself?"

"A little, but I didn't know anything about his finances. My sister made it very clear that it was none of my business since I'd, and these were her words, 'abandoned them for my fancy life in Boston.'"

"You're aware that the house you quitclaimed to your sister was mortgaged to the amount of its worth?"

"That I quitclaimed? What does that mean? My grandfather's house?"

"The form you signed that gave your sister full ownership is called a quitclaim deed," explained Decker.

What the fuck? "I didn't sign any form."

Rile stood and walked over to a bag he'd left on the table near the front door. He pulled out several pieces of paper, rifled through them, and handed one to me.

"That isn't my signature," I said, looking over the form I'd never seen before. "It isn't even close." I was seething. Sybil forged my signature? I'd gone through all my savings to pay my grandfather's bills, and while that was happening, she was mortgaging his house. That bitch. That selfish, damn bitch.

Decker took the paper. "It was notarized."

"That may be, but that isn't my signature. Isn't it obvious that Sybil got someone to notarize it for her so she could do whatever she damn well pleased?" I stood and snatched the paper from his hand.

"What's up?" he asked.

"I've had it. I know this sounds callous, but I don't care who killed my sister. In the last few days, I've found out that I have no friends, my family has done nothing but lie to me, and the only real thing in my life is my music, and that was taken away from me too. I'm done."

"What does that mean?" asked Decker, not even trying to hide the hurt in his eyes.

"It means I want to go back to Boston, apply for jobs so I can keep my apartment, and forget about everything in Texas, just like I did nine years ago." I stormed off, hating that I'd just hurt Decker's feelings, but I'd known him less than a week. Besides, I'd all but offered him my virginity on a silver platter, and he hadn't been interested in actually fucking me.

I tossed the clothes I'd planned to wash back in the suitcase, went into the bathroom to gather my toiletries, and shoved them in as well. I closed the bag and wheeled it out of the bedroom.

When I got back out to the kitchen, Decker was there, but I didn't see Rile.

"Is this really what you want to do?" he asked.

"There was a reason I left all those years ago. I don't belong here. I never have."

"I see."

"I'm sorry, Decker. You've done so much for me, and I appreciate it, but it's time for me to go home. You and your friends know far more about my life than I ever have, so you don't need me to help you figure out who killed my sister."

I hung my head when tears filled my eyes and ran down my cheeks. Decker put his arms around me and pulled me against him.

I started to laugh even though nothing I was about to say was funny. "You know what's crazy? I can't even afford the plane ticket home. And as far as making arrangements for Sybil's funeral and burial, I can't pay for those either. I have one more paycheck coming, and that will have to cover the rent on an apartment I won't be able to afford after this month unless I can get a job.

That's what I need to do. I need to go home and find a job, but I can't, can I?"

"If you truly want to go back to Boston, I'll take care of the cost of the plane ticket."

"Thanks for the offer, Decker, but I won't let you do that. I let Adler pay for too many things for too long. I can't even begin to wrap my head around what the hell was really going on with him. No. There's only one person who can help me right now, and it's damn time he started. I'm going to pay my father a visit, only this time, I'm not asking for a meeting, I'm just showing up. And it won't be after hours either. He's ashamed of me? Doesn't want anyone to know he has a kid? Tough shit. He's got billions; he can give me a couple thousand to tide me over." Maybe I should ask for more, enough to get out of town, pack up my apartment, and disappear for a while. I'd always wanted to go to Greece.

"It isn't a good idea to confront your father right now."

"Why…is he going to kill me?"

"Don't do this, Mila," Decker implored. "If you won't stay, let me take care of your expenses for a while."

28

Decker

Once I'd caught my breath after Mila's announcement that she was going "home" and wanted to forget about everything in Texas—including me, evidently—I tried to unscramble the thoughts racing through my head.

It hadn't occurred to me that she'd up and leave so quickly, particularly since I'd hoped to talk her into never going back.

Setting that aside, my first priority had to be Mila's safety. If she returned to Boston now, the only way I could protect her would be to go with her.

It wouldn't be completely out of the question. I could still work this investigation from there, especially since Rile, Edge, and Grinder were here.

"I'll go with you."

"*What? No!* Now you sound just like Adler."

Jesus, this woman was giving me some mighty swift kicks to the gut. I walked over and boxed her in between the kitchen counter and me. "First of all, I am nothing like Adler."

She looked down at the floor rather than at me. "I know you're not."

"Second, you may want to walk away from what's happened in the last week of your life, rewind the clock, but that doesn't mean you can. Whether you want to face the reality of your situation or not, you're in danger. Someone killed your sister. Whoever that person is, was looking for something, and until they find it, they're going to keep looking."

"I don't have what they're looking for."

"Are you sure? And, do you think it'll matter? Maybe Sybil didn't have it either."

My phone vibrated in my pocket. As much as I didn't want to turn my attention away from Mila, there were too many irons in the fire for me to continue ignoring calls. I pulled it out and saw a text from Edge.

Headed toward Austin.

Jesus. What was Adler up to now?

"Call Adler," I said, setting my phone down on the counter.

"Why?"

"Because enough time has passed without any word from him."

"What should I say?"

"Ask him where he is." I doubted Adler would answer Mila's call, but it was worth a shot. "If he says he's still in Texas, tell him you want to meet." It was a long shot, but if the man was headed to confront Judd—or worse—maybe we could waylay him.

Mila's eyes opened wide.

"You won't be alone."

She nodded and pulled her phone out of her bag. I stood close so I could hear the conversation if Adler answered.

"Mila? Where are you?" Adler said before I even heard the phone ring on the other end. I nodded when Mila looked at me.

"I'm at King-Alexander Ranch. Where are you? I didn't hear anything from you."

"I'm back in Boston, Mila. I went to Bluebell Creek. You never answered my calls or texts, so what choice did I have?"

Shit, I swore silently. So much for waylaying him.

"I didn't get any messages from you, Adler."

"Right. You've been pushing me away for years, and yet you practically fell into a stranger's arms. Maybe you should ask him about my messages. My guess is he deleted them before you saw them."

I quickly wrote something on a piece of paper and pointed to it. When Mila raised her eyebrows, I nodded.

"What about Sybil, Adler?"

"I'm sorry your sister is gone, Mila, but I don't know what you want me to do. I came to Bluebell Creek to meet you, help you make arrangements for her funeral, and the people in the cemetery office said they hadn't seen or heard from you."

"Adler, please. Did you really think I wouldn't find out about the two of you?"

Mila bit her lower lip as we waited for Adler to come up with a response.

We heard him sigh. "I really wanted to spare you this, Mila, and I'm sorry to tell you this over the phone, but your sister came to me when I was in town for your grandfather's funeral. She said she was in trouble and knew she couldn't come to you for help."

"What kind of trouble?"

"Gambling debts. Again, I wanted to spare you, so I agreed to help her. I've been trying to get her into a Gamblers' Anonymous program, but all she did was continue to ring up more debt. I finally had to cut her off." He sighed again. "I want you to know that I spoke with the sheriff about this. I suggested that one lead into her murder might be the people she owed money to."

I wrote another note.

"Murder, Adler? What makes you think Sybil was

murdered? There was an accident..."

"*Mila!*" he gasped. "I was certain the sheriff told you."

I made a motion for her to wrap it up.

"Um, Adler, I...uh...need to go. I'll...uh...call you back. I need to call the sheriff."

"Don't do that, Mila. Let me call him first to see if they have any leads."

Her forehead scrunched. "I can ask that same question, Adler."

"Sweetheart, let me handle this for you."

I wanted to reach through the phone and strangle the *sonuvabitch*. Let him handle this? He's probably the one who arranged for Sybil's murder. I made another motion, this time simulating a throat cutting.

"I have to go, Adler. Thank you for the information." I watched as Mila pressed the button to end the call and then double-checked to make sure the call had disconnected.

"Do you think there's any truth to what he said?"

"We know he's not in Boston. I'd say that if he began with a lie, it's likely he continued that way."

"Can you call the sheriff?"

I was already taking my phone out to do so.

"Did you have a meeting with Adler Livingston?" I

asked when Mac answered.

"A meeting?"

"A conversation?"

"A conversation?" the sheriff repeated.

"Come on, Mac. I don't have time for this bullshit."

"I had one conversation with Adler Livingston, at the office while you were with Mila Knight."

"He didn't contact you suggesting that Sybil Knight may have been killed by people she owed money to?"

"Decker, what's this about?"

"Answer the question, Mac."

"No."

"Did you, at any time, tell Adler Livingston that Sybil Knight was murdered?"

"Give me a damn break, Deck."

"Just making sure, Mac."

"Anything else?"

"Not for now."

"Have you and your crew figured out who killed her yet?"

"I don't have a crew, Mac, but you do. What leads do you have?"

Mac laughed and ended the call.

"The sheriff isn't investigating my sister's murder?"

"Of course he is. He's also aware that we're running our own investigation and that we can employ other…

tactics."

"What do you think Adler will do now?"

"No idea, but Edge and Grinder will prevent him from doing anything too damaging."

"Like what?"

"Confronting your father."

Mila gave a little shrug of her shoulder and looked out the window.

"What do you want to do, sweetheart?"

"What do you mean?"

"Boston?"

"It's where I live, Decker."

"Are you ready to go back now?"

She didn't answer right away, which I saw as a good sign.

"You know what I'd really like to do?"

I smiled and shook my head. If it had anything to do with us getting naked, I was all in.

"Rile said our old house is being held in trust for me."

"That's right."

"I'd like to go see it."

"Let's go."

29

Mila

As Decker turned off the highway and onto the dirt road, memories came flooding back to me. I remembered our mother driving Sybil and me home from school every day and how I'd hold my breath, hoping I'd see my father's car in the yard. I never did; not in the middle of the afternoon. Most nights, I was in bed before he got home.

I remembered a table in the kitchen where Sybil and I would do our homework while our mother fixed dinner. I could count on one hand the number of times my father ate with us. He was even gone on the weekends.

When Decker pulled up to the white clapboard house, it took my breath away. How had I forgotten how much I'd loved living here?

It looked pretty rough; the lawn near the house hadn't been mowed in years. The bushes were overgrown, and the back porch looked like it was collapsing. The windows on the first level were boarded up, but the upstairs ones in the dormers, weren't. The front of the house didn't look like it was in as bad shape as the back, and the black shutters looked as though all they'd need was a fresh coat of paint.

"Do you want to go inside?" Decker asked.

"Can we?"

"It's your house, sweetheart."

"Yes. I'd like to."

"Let's go."

I waited for Decker to come around to my side of the truck. "I'm nervous," I admitted.

"One thing to keep in mind is critters may have taken up residence."

"Right," I said as we walked up to the front door.

Decker reached out to open it, but it was locked. I picked up the partially broken pot sitting on the front porch, brushed away the dry dirt, and found the key I remembered had always been hidden there.

Decker stomped his way inside, I guessed to scare away any of those critters he'd mentioned. It was dark with the boards over the windows, but when I, like Decker, shined the light from my phone in the front room, I gasped. It all looked the same as I remembered it on the day my mother, my sister, and I had left. Maybe it was because it was dark, but it didn't look as dilapidated as the outside had.

I took a few more steps and peeked around the corner, holding my breath. "Oh my God, it's still here," I gasped, shining the light on the baby grand piano where I'd taken my first lesson.

"Let's get some light in here," Decker said, going back out the front door. Moments later, I heard the wood crack as he pulled the thin boards from the three front windows. The room was immediately flooded with light. I lifted the keylid, and sat down on the bench, tentatively pressing my fingers to the keys.

I'd expected it to be out of tune, but it wasn't as far gone as I thought it would be.

Bringing both hands to the keys, I began to play. I played and played and played, pounding out every piece of music I knew by heart. Somewhere in the back of my mind, I could hear Decker moving about the house, removing boards, opening windows, perhaps to air it out. I should probably stop and help, but as soon as I finished one piece, I told myself I'd just play one more.

Only when I felt Decker standing behind me did I move my hands from the keys.

"Don't stop," he murmured.

"I know it needs a good tuning, but I love this piano. I couldn't resist."

"It sounded beautiful."

I turned on the bench and looked around the room. "It's like it was frozen in time."

"Would you like to take a look around?"

I stood and took Decker's extended hand, so anxious to see the other rooms of the house.

We walked through the formal dining room that was only used for holiday meals, and into the farmhouse kitchen. There was a wooden ladder in the corner that neither I nor Sybil had ever been allowed to climb. Our mother used it to reach things in the row of cabinets that butted up against the ceiling.

The oversized sink looked out on the orchard where peaches, plums, pomegranates, figs, pears, and apples grew. Beyond it, were rows and rows of blackberries, all horribly overgrown.

"I thought I'd check out the barn," said Decker from behind me. "I've been in all the rooms. I didn't see any sign of wildlife."

I nodded as I ran my hands over the kitchen counters. Being here made me miss my mother so much more than the last time I'd visited my grandfather's house. Maybe because I always thought of it as his, whereas this was my mother's house. Not my father's; he was never here. That he'd made us leave it, was heartbreaking. Especially considering it didn't appear that anyone had lived here after we left.

The same table sat in what would probably be called a breakfast nook now. I walked out of the kitchen and to the stairway.

Upstairs there were four bedrooms. Sybil and I had had our own in this house. We'd had to share when we moved in with our grandfather. My room looked exactly the same as it had the day we left. It had the same blue toile wallpaper and the white hobnail cotton bedspread. It was dusty, of course, but otherwise, it was just as I remembered.

"Was this your room?" Decker asked from the door-way.

"It was." I pointed to the chair that sat next to the dormer window. "I used to sit there and read."

"I can see you there."

I ran my hand over the old-fashioned dresser and looked into the mirror that hung above it. The last time I'd seen my reflection in it, I was seven years old. I'd been barely tall enough to see myself.

"Why did he make us leave?"

"I wish I knew," Decker answered, coming to stand behind me.

"You're a handsome man," I said, looking at his reflection next to mine. I shuddered as I watched him lean down and kiss beneath my ear, my neck, up to my cheek. It was the sexiest thing I'd ever seen.

"You belong here," he murmured. "This house suits you."

I turned in his arms. "Texas isn't my home anymore, Decker. I don't think it has been since the day we left this house."

He opened his mouth to say something, but closed it when the phone in his pocket rang.

"It's the medical examiner," he told me before he accepted the call.

"Hey, Doc. What can I do for you?"

I was close enough that I could hear the man's response.

"I've completed the autopsy, Decker, and I found something you should see. How soon can you be here?"

Something we should see? Oh, God. What did that mean?

"I don't know, maybe an hour?"

"Sooner the better, Deck."

"We can leave now," I told him when the call ended.

"Do you want to look at any of the other bedrooms first?"

"No. They weren't mine."

He nodded as if he understood. "There isn't much to see in the barn."

"I don't remember ever being in there."

Decker put his hands on my shoulders. "While the house doesn't appear like anyone's been in it. I can't say the same about the barn."

"No?"

"There are three different sets of footprints that all look recent."

I didn't like the look on Decker's face. "Does one set look like they belong to a woman?"

"They do."

"What do you want to do?"

"I'll give Rile a call on our way to see the medical examiner and then mention it to Mac when we get there."

30

Decker

While the grandfather's house had been trashed, it wasn't the crime scene. This was. The barn anyway. Edge hadn't said anything about Adler entering either the house or the barn, so my guess was all three sets of footprints had been left the night Sybil was murdered.

"Hello, my friend."

I rolled my eyes. "Rile, we're over at Mila's house. There are footprints in the barn that I need someone to take a look at. The medical examiner called, and there's something he wants me to see."

"Understood."

"Are Edge and Grinder still in Austin?"

"They're on their way back. Adler Livingston was close to Knighthawk headquarters and then abruptly changed course and went to the airport. Grinder confirmed he got on a plane headed to Boston."

"Good," I muttered, not at all surprised. Adler needed to regroup, and I knew exactly whom with. "Where's Casper?"

"On her way to Boston as well. She'll land within the hour."

I smiled. Maybe being part of this team wasn't so bad, after all.

"I'll have the boys go directly to the barn."

"Thanks, Rile."

"Adler is on his way back to Boston," I repeated to Mila. "An agent is also on her way there."

"She'll follow him?"

"Yes. She'll be there before he is."

"Her name is Casper?"

"Yes. Her code name."

"Why?"

"My understanding is she's exceptionally good at silent approaches followed by vanishing with graceful stealth."

"Wow."

"Not my words, by the way. I read it in her dossier."

"Decker, thank you for getting here so quickly," said the medical examiner, meeting us near the building's entrance.

"What did you want me to see?"

He looked over at Mila and then back at me.

"It's fine," I assured him.

The man nodded, pulled an evidence bag out of his pocket, and held it up.

"What is that?" I asked.

"A flash drive."

"Where did you find it?"

The medical examiner leaned in close. "Our victim ingested it."

"What's on it?"

He shrugged. "Mac said you should have the first look."

"Is Mac here?"

"He left shortly after I spoke with you."

I put my hand on the medical examiner's shoulder. "Thanks, Doc. Anything else I need to know?"

"Nothing else unexpected."

"Good."

"Did he say Sybil ingested it?" Mila asked once we were back outside.

"I wasn't sure if you heard him."

"She swallowed it?"

"That's right."

"Do you think that's what whoever killed her was looking for?"

"I do." I'd also lay odds that it was what Adler was looking for too.

"What do you think is on it?"

I had no idea, but my gut was telling me that I needed to find out without Mila being present.

I stopped at the main house instead of going straight to my place.

"I'm going to take this in to Rile. I'll be right back."

"Don't you want to see what's on it?"

"I do, but I'd like Rile to take a look first."

Mila's brow furrowed. "Why?"

I scrubbed my face with my hand. "Because I don't know what it is."

Mila turned away from me. "All you have to say is that you're afraid whatever it is, is something I shouldn't see. Isn't that what's really going on here?"

"Yes."

I put the truck back in gear and drove the rest of the way to my house.

"I'm going to start my laundry," Mila told me, pulling the carry-on bag we'd left in the kitchen behind her.

I went into the office, closed the door, and then attached the drive to the laptop I kept off the main servers. If this thing was set up to do any kind of data damage, it would be minimal and contained. As I waited for it to load, I wondered if it had been in Sybil's stomach too long and was damaged.

I held my breath as I saw it spin up. The flash drive contained two folders, both named by year. The first was of the same year as the divorce and Sybil's surgery. The second was from nine years ago.

I took a deep breath and opened the most recent date; inside was an MP4 file. I scrubbed my face with my hand and opened the file.

The first thing I saw was a grainy image of what I guessed was Mila waiting for the elevator. It went on for five minutes, without any audio. I watched as the young woman turned and walked out of the camera's view.

There were a few seconds of nothing but black which then cut directly to the stairwell. I held my breath again, watching as the scene Mila had described, played out on my computer screen. I stood, unable to sit still, but kept my eyes on the screen. This part contained audio, which only made it more horrific.

When Mila's father rushed into the scene, I leaned forward and increased the volume.

As Mila had said, he screamed at her to go to her office and wait. The video wasn't as grainy as that of her waiting for the elevator, but it was enough so I couldn't see her face, and for that, I was glad.

Mila's father grabbed the man by the throat and ripped the ski mask from his head.

The man laughed, followed by "She looks just like her—" Judd swung and hit the man in the mouth. He stumbled backward, but that didn't stop him. "Just like her mother. Just like her. A slut born of a slut."

Judd grabbed him again and held him by the throat. "The difference is, you made her mother a slut."

"Difference?" The man cackled. "It was the best revenge of all, that you didn't believe her. I blew up your fucking miserable life, and the daughter you thought was yours..."

It was Judd's turn to laugh. "You're wrong. I knew from the minute she was born that Sybil wasn't mine."

"You're the same fucking liar you've always been, Knight."

I watched as Judd pummeled the man and then pushed him out of the frame; the screen went black.

Fighting back the bile that came up in my throat, I wiped my mouth with my shirt sleeve. If Sybil had swallowed the flash drive in an effort to keep her killer from getting his hands on it, it was likely she'd seen the video.

I closed the file and opened the second folder. Inside were over two hundred jpg photo files, all dated ten days before I found Sybil dying on the side of the road—which meant she'd somehow gotten her hands on the original files and photographed them.

I opened and zoomed in on the first one, which was a cover sheet for a patent application. Randomly opening several more, I saw some contained text, others drawings. Finally, I clicked on and opened the only document that mattered—the page that would prove that the original patents were prepared to be filed by Marshall Livingston.

A quick online search provided proof of the second half of what I assumed. United States Patent URE47,825 listed the inventor as Knight, Judson A, and the Assignee, Knighthawk Corporation, Austin, Texas.

It wasn't difficult for me to piece together a theory as to what had got Sybil killed. She'd somehow gotten her hands on not just the documents that proved Judd Knight had stolen Livingston's designs, but also the video of Mila's attack.

The unanswered questions now were, had she found this evidence on her own and attempted to blackmail either her father or Livingston, or both? And which one killed her for it?

What I did know for certain, though, was that Adler Livingston's father, Marshall, was the man who'd attacked Mila. Which brought up yet another question. How much did Adler know?

31

Mila

If I'd thought I felt like I was ready to crawl out of my skin before, it was nothing compared to how I felt now. Decker had been in the office for almost an hour. That had to mean the flash drive wasn't damaged when Sybil swallowed it and that there was something significant on it. Right? Would he have been in there that long if there wasn't? I felt weird hanging out in the kitchen, so I walked over to the living room and pulled a book from the shelf.

It was one I'd noticed the first time I perused his collection, and was fascinated that it was one of only a couple of fiction books mixed in with several historical and ranching non-fiction hardbacks.

The title was *The Confessions of Max Tivoli*. It was about a man whose mind ages normally, but is born with the withered body of a seventy-year-old. As his body ages in reverse, he manages to cross paths with a woman who captures his heart three different times— giving him three chances for true love.

A number of theories ran through my mind about why Decker would own such a book. First, and most unlikely, was that he was a hopeless romantic. Second was that someone had given it to him as a gift, which I found equally unlikely. And third, perhaps the books on his shelves were merely for show and he didn't realize he had it.

I sat on the sofa, opened the cover, and was shocked to see that it was signed with a personal message to him from the author.

Decker—
Pay attention the first time. Don't make the
same mistakes I did.
—A Greer

I turned to the first page and soon was so mesmerized, I didn't hear Decker walk up behind me.

"Hi," I said, setting the book down and turning to move my legs so he could sit beside me.

"Good book," he commented when I set it on the coffee table.

"Are you asking or saying?"

He smiled. "Saying."

"It is good. Very good, in fact." I picked it back up.

"Mila…"

"What's on the flash drive, Decker?"

"A couple of things."

I stood and put the book back on the shelf. "Just tell me." If I sounded irritated, I was. Why tell me there was something on it if he didn't intend to tell me what it was?

"Sybil is your half-sister, as well as Adler's."

"Okay," I whispered, clutching the back of the nearest chair.

"Come sit down."

When I did, Decker put his arm around me. "This will be more difficult."

"Go ahead."

"What's on the drive confirms that Adler's father is the man who attacked you in the stairwell."

I closed my eyes and let my head drop back against Decker's arm. This wasn't unexpected news, particularly after he'd told me that Marshall and my father had been roommates in college.

"Let's go back to Sybil being my half-sister. Do you think she was aware of it?"

"There's no way of knowing how long she knew before her death, but it might offer some explanation as to why she and Adler were spending time together."

I nodded. "What else was on it?"

"Proof that Livingston developed technology your father took credit for. Somehow, Judd managed to file the patents with himself listed as the inventor rather than Adler's father. The original drawings as well as the technical data that was on the flash drive essentially prove your father stole the technology. That's an over-simplification."

"Not that I have any reason to defend my father, but is it possible he purchased the technology?"

Decker shook his head. "If that were the case, Livingston would have been listed as the inventor and your father and/or his company would be listed as the assignee."

"Do you think he killed Sybil?"

"I don't know. There's an equal chance it was Livingston."

"Sybil swallowed the flash drive rather than give it to her killer." It should've shocked me, didn't. It was like I'd become immune to all the crazy shit swirling around me.

"That's right," Decker murmured, nodding.

"Marshall wouldn't want proof that he attacked me exposed. My father wouldn't want anyone to have proof that he was a thief."

"Based on what I read, Livingston stood the chance of being compensated in the billions if he were able to prove the inventions were his."

"You keep saying Livingston. I'm not going to fall apart if I hear his name, Decker. I just said it myself."

"That isn't why."

"Why, then?"

"It humanizes him."

"I see. What are you planning to do, Decker?"

"While we're able to resolve certain things from what was on the drive, there are many more questions that remain unanswered."

"Who killed Sybil?"

"Yes. Also, there's the question of your parents' divorce."

"What of it?" My mother was dead. What difference would anything that happened with their marriage make now?

"Keep in mind that I am only theorizing at this point."

"I'm aware of that, Decker." I stood and walked back over to the bookcase, my fists clenched tightly. I was so angry I was shaking, but who was I mad at? My father? Sybil? Adler? Marshall? Or was I angry at Decker? "I'd appreciate it if you'd get to the point."

He stood too. "Okay. Here's the point, Mila. Based on the argument your father had with Marshall after he instructed you to go up to his office and wait for him, I believe there's a reasonable chance he raped your mother."

"'She looks just like her—' He was talking about my mother."

"There was something else he said, 'The best revenge of all was that you didn't believe her.' Marshall went on to say that he blew up your father's life."

"You're thinking that my father realized Sybil wasn't his when she needed a blood transfusion?"

"Adds up." Decker stepped closer to me, and I stepped back. "What's going on, Mila?"

I didn't know. I couldn't explain why, but the idea of Decker touching me made my skin crawl. "I'd like to be alone," I said, wrapping my arms tightly around myself. "Maybe go back to the old house."

"Okay. We can do that. I'd like to meet with Rile first."

I turned my back to him. "Okay."

"Mila?"

"It's a lot to process, Decker."

32

Adler

"*Who in the hell are you?*" I said to the woman sitting on the arm of my sofa when I walked into my apartment and flipped on the light.

"I'm here to talk about Sybil Knight's murder, Adler," the woman said, calm as she fucking could be.

"How did you get in here?"

"Think you're the only person who knows how to break and enter?" She unfolded her arms as she spoke, revealing a gun.

I threw my arms up and motioned toward the gun. "*Whoa, that* is not necessary. *Who the fuck are you?*"

The woman stood and walked over to me. "Who I am isn't important. What's important is I don't like swearing, so you'll stop that now."

I ran my hand through my hair. With or without a gun, this woman was scary as shit. Didn't help that she was dressed all in black leather in the middle of fucking July. "What do you want?"

"I already told you. You're going to tell me everything you know about Sybil Knight's murder."

"I don't know shit about Sybil Knight."

Before I had time to blink, the crazy bitch pistol-whipped me, hitting me square in the jaw.

"Jesus," I yelled, bringing my hand up to my mouth. "I'm bleeding."

"I'm getting tired of repeating myself, Adler. I said, I don't like swearing." She leaned into me when she said it, and I backed into the kitchen island. "Sit!" she barked, motioning to the closest stool and taking another step forward.

I held up my hands again. "Okay. I'm sitting."

"Put your hands behind your back."

"Why?"

The woman scrunched her eyes.

"Okay. Look. Hands behind back." I peered over my shoulder and saw her pull out a pair of handcuffs that she promptly put on my wrists. "Are you a cop?"

The woman laughed, which only scared me more.

"If I were a cop, you'd have a much better night than you're gonna have."

33

Decker

"Casper's interrogating Adler Livingston presently," Rile said with a twinkle in his eye.

I stepped to the side so he could see that Mila was with me.

"Are Edge and Grinder here?"

"Yes," he answered at the same time both men in question joined us in the kitchen.

"I was able to review the contents of the flash drive the medical examiner found in Sybil Knight's stomach."

Grinder's eyes opened wide, and he looked around me at Mila.

"Mila has been briefed on its contents." I walked into the main dining room and motioned for her to join me. I reached out to put my hand on her shoulder, and she jerked away from me. It stunned me so much that I stood frozen, looking into her eyes. "Talk to me, Mila. Tell me why you just did that," I said quietly enough that only she could hear me.

She took another step back. "I don't know."

I looked down at the floor and then back up at her. "Do you want to be in this meeting? I'll warn you that

I'm not going to pull any punches if you are. I need to tell the guys everything I told you, along with everything I didn't. That includes reviewing the surveillance recordings from the night you were attacked."

"I'll stay."

"You're sure?"

"I just said I'd stay."

"Have a seat." I didn't know what the hell was going on with her, but right now, I had to brief the team, especially since Casper was with Adler. As soon as Rile said she was, I began compiling a mental list of things she could question him about.

"I've forwarded the contents of the flash drive to each of you," I said when the men joined Mila and me at the table.

"Let's start with the video."

Grinder looked at me and then at Mila a second time, and it pissed me off. "Yes, Grinder, I am aware Mila is here. It was her choice to stay or leave. She chose to stay. Any further questions?"

"Sorry, Deck," said Grinder, holding up his hands.

"There's audio, Mila."

Her eyes were as wide as Grinder's had been.

I heard a chair push back and saw Grinder getting up from the table. "You're a fucking wanker," he spat.

That wasn't the worst of it. When the man held his hand out to Mila, she took it. No flinch. No hesitation. They both walked out of the room.

"Not a fucking word," I said to Edge, and then turned to look at Rile, whose eyes were hooded.

"Both of you go ahead and watch it. You can review the patent documents as well. If you have any questions, you can ask me when I get back."

I stormed through the kitchen and out the back door. I didn't know where Grinder took Mila, and I didn't care. I needed to get the fuck out of there before I lost my temper completely.

Since when was I the fucking bad guy? I'd asked Mila if she wanted to stay, and she'd said yes. In fact, she'd snapped at me when I asked if she was sure. And then, after flinching away from me, she took Grinder's hand like it was no big deal.

That, right there, was like a knife to my chest. I stalked into the office, grabbed the key to the Bummer, and walked through the barn to where we kept it.

I threw open the alley doors, got in, and started it up. Thank God, Boon had been driving it. If it hadn't turned over, I might've smashed it to smithereens. Not that it would've been possible. This thing was built like a tank, mainly because, in part, it was one.

I took off through the closest pasture, back to the fire road where I could open the Bummer all the way up. I'd forgotten how fun this thing was to drive; the last time I had, it was because some fucking English footballers had figured out how to temporarily disable the ranch's security system along with all of the vehicles they'd known about, and then kidnapped a woman who Z had moved here to keep her safe.

They sure as shit hadn't known about the Bummer, nor did they know that even though they'd thrown a wrench in the system Burns and I had put in place, we had backups that no one could fuck with.

The kidnappers had ended up with bullets in their brains, the woman was now married to a former MI6 agent, and everyone lived happily ever after.

That was when Quint met his wife, too. For the second time in a handful of days, I felt the absence of my best friend. It wasn't like we were joined at the hip, but if there was ever a time I needed his advice, now was it.

As I drove, I went over and over what had transpired between Mila and me in the last couple of hours.

After watching the surveillance tape of her attack, and then sorting through the patent files, I'd spent fifteen minutes thinking over the best way to tell her what I'd seen, that I knew who her attacker had been, and that Sybil wasn't her father's child.

Somehow, I'd gotten it so wrong that she couldn't stand for me to touch her. What though? What had I said? How had I said it?

I thought back over her reaction to each piece of information I'd presented her with. She'd been shocked, but she continued asking questions. It was when I mentioned her parents' divorce and my theory about what had caused it, that she first appeared angry.

The Bummer hit a big bump right when I crested a rise, sending it airborne. The back three rows of seats rattled around, since they weren't all that secure, to begin with, but my beloved Frankenstein vehicle landed smooth as butter and kept right on going.

This wasn't the first vehicle Quint and I had built. We'd started out taking one of the tractors apart and reassembling it so it looked more like a cross between a lawnmower and a go-cart. It was when I decided to make it radio-operated that Z took notice.

"Show me how it works," he'd said to my then-fifteen-year-old self.

I'd showed him, and even though there were things I hadn't figured out how to make work yet, Z had still been impressed.

The following summer, he took Quint and me on a road trip to California. We'd pulled that damn modified tractor all the way to the Central Coast. When we arrived, an old man came out on the porch of one of the coolest houses I'd ever seen.

When we got out of the truck, Z had put his hand on my shoulder. "This is the boy I've been telling you about."

The man descended the steps so slowly, I thought maybe Quint and I should help him. When he reached the bottom, he walked around the trailer, looking at the tractor. He studied it for a few minutes and then walked over to where Quint and I waited with Z.

"My name is Laird Butler," the man had said. "Although I'm also known as Burns."

I remembered shaking the man's hand, and then him saying, "Come with me, young man. You and I are going to figure out what else we can control by radio."

At first, I felt bad that Burns hadn't said anything to Quint, but later that night, before we went to sleep in the guest house the Butler family had invited us to stay in, Quint reassured me.

"I'd be pissed if he asked how you reassembled the chassis, because I'm the one who did that. Mr. Butler wasn't interested in that. He wanted to know how you'd rigged the remote."

After a few days, Z told me that he and Quint were heading back to Texas and that I'd be staying on for two more weeks, finishing a project that Burns and I had started.

It was easy now to look back and see what a great opportunity Z had given me. Then, it was a different story. I'd gotten it in my head that Z was leaving me there. Abandoning me. I couldn't have been more wrong, but it took Burns and his wife to convince me of that.

Three days later, I was in the basement of the Butler's house where Burns and I were working on one of our projects, when I heard a knock on the door. Burns had hollered to whoever it was to come in, and in walked Z.

I didn't see Burns leave the room, but he had. Z came over and sat across the work table from me, handing me a piece of paper.

"What is this?" I'd asked.

"Adoption papers."

A few weeks later, Z took me to the Hays County Courthouse and made me his son. The only other person who knew about it was Quint, and I told him that I wanted to keep it between the three of us. Z hadn't done it so anyone would think what a great guy he was. He'd done it because he wanted me to know that he'd never leave me behind.

My legal name after that day became Decker Ashford Alexander, but I'd always used Ashford as my last name. Z respected my decision, because that's the kind of man he is.

I stopped the Bummer, wiped the tears from my eyes, and looked over at the two cell phones that I'd thrown on the passenger seat. Maybe I couldn't—or wouldn't—contact Quint. The man was on his honeymoon. But I sure as hell could call Z.

34

Mila

"Are you okay?" Grinder asked as he drove me back over to the old house.

"Yes and no. I know none of this is Decker's fault. I don't know why I got so upset with him."

"Maybe because he was a damn wanker," Grinder muttered, looking out the driver's side window.

"He really did ask me if I was sure I wanted to stay, and I told him I did."

"He shouldn't have asked in the first place."

I understood Grinder's thinking, but I disagreed. If Decker hadn't, I would've been even angrier.

"I'm sorry about interrupting your meeting."

"Not a problem. Are you sure you'll be okay on your own here?"

"Definitely." While I hadn't decided what I'd do about the property, I didn't have to yet. It wouldn't be mine for four more years, and I couldn't think that far ahead.

As soon as I could, I intended to return to my life in Boston. I'd find a job, a new apartment, and move on from this in the same way I'd moved on nine years ago when I'd originally gone to Massachusetts.

While I'd gotten lazy about spending time with friends other than Adler, I did have them. Lots of them were from the music program. Maybe one could even help me get a job.

I supposed the bank would contact me about my grandfather's house, since I was the only remaining heir. Given it was mortgaged for more than it was worth, they'd either take it over or I'd have to sell it, and I could handle either from Boston.

Whether it was my father or Marshall Livingston, or even Adler, who had killed Sybil, I knew Decker and the Invincibles would see to it that they were brought to justice.

In the meantime, I needed money, and I intended to get it.

I waved as Grinder drove off. There were still several hours of daylight that I could use to start cleaning the place up. In fact, the first thing I'd do would be to call and get the utilities turned back on.

Wait. That would be the second thing I did. First, I'd call my father.

Nine years ago, my hand shook when I dialed the number that I'd had to look up. Not this time.

"I'm calling for Judd Knight," I said when the operator said, "Knighthawk, how may I help you?"

"This is Mila Knight. I'm calling for my father."

"Your father?"

"Yes, ma'am. Judd Knight. My father."

"One moment please."

I was on hold for several minutes, but I didn't care.

"Hello, Miss Knight. This is Kitty, Mr. Knight's assistant. Is there something I can help you with, dear?"

"You sure can, Kitty. Get my fucking father on the phone."

The woman cleared her throat. "One moment. I'll see if he's available."

I sat on the steps of the front porch and lifted my face to the sun, remembering days when my mother and I would do the same thing.

"Mila."

"Judd."

"Not funny."

"Did you expect me to call you Dad?"

"Where are you, Mila?"

"I'm at my house. The one that becomes mine when I'm thirty."

"You found out about that. I can't say I'm surprised."

"That's what I'm calling about. In part, anyway. I need money."

"I see."

"As I'm sure you know, I paid off Granddaddy's bills, and Sybil's too. You know, my *sister*, Sybil."

"That's enough, Mila."

I laughed. "Oh, I'm just getting started. Want to know how to get me to stop? Twenty-five thousand dollars should do it."

"Is that all?"

"I'm not greedy, Judd. I just need enough to get back on my feet. The same day I got a call saying my *sister* was dead, I lost my job. And, as it turns out, the apartment building I live in happens to be owned by the man who tried to rape me when I was seventeen years old. You remember, right? Marshall Livingston? Yeah, I live in a building he owns. Ironic, isn't it?"

"Is there a reason you think I would give you twenty-five grand? After all, I did give you a house."

"I'm sure you had an ulterior motive for that particular gift, like maybe keeping it out of my mother's hands. As far as why you'd give me the money I'm asking for, I have billions of reasons. *Billions* and *billions* of them."

He chuckled at my accusation about the house, but his tone changed with my threat. "Come to the office and we'll talk."

"I don't think so, *Daddy*. Remember what happened the last time I was there? You can wire the money. I'll expect it tomorrow."

I ended the call, stood, and went inside. That hadn't been as hard as I thought it would be.

The next call I made was to the electric company, who, after keeping me on hold for almost fifteen minutes, told me that according to their records, the power was on at the house.

I walked over and flipped a switch. "Nope," I told the woman.

"Have you tried the circuit breaker?"

"The circuit breaker? Where would that be?"

"I couldn't say, miss, but I could schedule someone to come out and take a look next week."

"I'll see if I can find it. If not, I'll call you back."

I remembered the electrical panel at my grandfather's house was in the garage. This house didn't have a garage. It had a basement, though. I had no idea why I remembered that, but I did. It was unusual for houses in Texas to have them, another fact I had no idea how I knew.

Grabbing my phone, I pried open the door that was between the kitchen and the back porch, and then remembered the porch was partially collapsed. I went back inside and out the front of the house. The double doors that led to the basement were around the back, closer to where the garden had been. I vaguely remembered that my mother kept root vegetables we'd grown down there because they'd last longer.

I was stunned at the random memories that continued flooding back to me.

The doors I thought might be hard to open, did so very easily. Shining the light from my phone ahead of me, I walked down the stone steps.

When I got to the bottom, I moved my phone in a semi-circle. It was creepier down here than I remembered, probably because I'd never been down here without any light.

I also didn't remember it being this big. At first glance, there was nothing resembling an electrical panel. There had to be a furnace, though, right? And a water heater? Maybe the panel I was looking for was in the same vicinity.

"Yes!" I exclaimed when I opened a door to my right and saw not only the furnace but, behind it, the electrical panel. I tucked my phone under my chin and pried the panel's cover off. At the very top, there was a breaker larger than the others. When I flipped it one way, my phone slipped and fell on the dirt floor. "Dammit," I mumbled and flipped the switch back the other way. I leaned down, picked up my phone, and shined it near the doorway. There was no switch, but there was a string hanging down. Who knew how old the light bulb in it might be, but it was worth a try.

"Yes!" I exclaimed again when the light went on.

Feeling very proud of myself, I pulled the string again to turn the light off and pointed my phone at the way back out.

I switched it off when I got close enough to the steps that the light from outside shone in.

Not only had I called my father and told him I needed money, which I thought he'd agreed to send—mainly because of my veiled threat—but I'd also turned my own electricity back on. That probably wouldn't seem like a big accomplishment to someone like Decker.

Decker. After being with him around the clock for the last few days, now that I wasn't, I missed him. Even I didn't understand my reaction to him earlier; it was totally illogical. One minute, I trusted him, wanted him, enjoyed being with him, all implicitly. The next, I was so angry, I couldn't stand the idea of him touching me.

What had he done wrong? Nothing. He'd been kind and loving, protective, and so fucking sexy that imagining him naked made me almost lose my footing.

I wondered if he and the rest of the Invincibles were still meeting. I smiled at the name I'd given them and his warning that they were an arrogant bunch and didn't need me pumping their already overinflated egos.

When I got to the top of the steps, I tucked my phone in the pocket of my shorts and closed the two doors. I pulled it back out and swiped the screen. I needed to call Decker and apologize. Looking at both, I wondered which of his numbers I should call first.

"Hello, Mila," I heard someone say from behind me at the same time he reached around and snatched the phone from my hand. "Remember me? We have some unfinished business."

I spun around and looked into eyes that looked so familiar. They were Adler's eyes, but he wasn't the man standing in front of me, sneering.

35

Adler

"Do you know how much money that bas—, man stole from our family? Billions." I told the woman who had been relentlessly questioning me for what felt like hours but was probably not even thirty minutes.

"Walk me through it, Adler. You and your father blackmailed Sybil Knight—"

"No! We didn't blackmail her. She needed money. We offered to pay her to get the information from her father that would prove my father should've been listed as the real inventor on Knighthawk's patents. That was it. It took her a few months, but about a week ago, she made contact and said she believed she found what we were looking for. I told my dad, thinking he'd tell me to make arrangements to get it from her, but he said he'd handle it himself."

The woman was studying something on her phone. She walked to the other side of the room, and I could hear voices but not what they were saying.

"*Jesus,*" I heard her mutter.

"What?" I asked, but she didn't respond. Whatever it was, held her attention for several more minutes. She opened the door that led to the outdoor patio and closed it behind her. When she came back, she looked even more pissed off than she'd been before.

"We're gonna start all over again, this time on a completely different subject, Adler. Now we're gonna talk about Mila Knight and what your sick *fuck* of a father did to her."

36

Decker

"What do you mean you left her there alone?" I was ready to tear my hair out. "Do you not understand that her sister was murdered for this?" I held up the flash drive. "It didn't occur to you that either Marshall Livingston or her own father might assume she has it since she was given her sister's effects? *Fuck!*"

Spinning around, I went back the way I came in. If I stayed another minute longer, I'd rip Grinder's damn face off. I pulled my phone from my pocket and swiped the screen. Mila's cell rang three times and then went to voicemail. Classic avoidance; she'd manually declined my call.

"Goddammit," I swore at the phone. Now wasn't the time for her to avoid me. I needed to know she was safe.

I climbed back into the Bummer, so pissed that I'd been two minutes away from her place when I decided to turn around and go back to the ranch. It would take me ten minutes to get back there if I took the fire road, fifteen on the highway.

"Decker!" I heard Edge yell right before I pulled away.

"What?"

"We put a tracker on Judd Knight's vehicle. He's at the house with Mila," Edge yelled.

"Go!" Grinder added. "We're right behind you."

Edge ran around to the other side of the Bummer, but he was too late; I'd already peeled away.

When I pulled in behind the barn, I cut the engine. From there, I could see Judd standing near the back of the house. He looked like he was in a conversation, and while I couldn't see whom with, I assumed it was Mila.

I ran as close to the side of the barn as I could, gun drawn. I'd have to cross in the yard out in the open, but if Judd saw me, at least he'd know I was near enough to get a clean shot off if he tried anything.

I took off running, and Judd saw me, but his reaction was one I didn't expect. I was close enough to see the terror that flashed in the man's eyes. Judd didn't want the person he was talking to, to know I was there.

When I got closer to the house, I stayed near the exterior wall where I could still see Judd—more importantly—I could hear him.

"Let her go, Livingston. It's me you want," he said, raising both his hands.

"*Fuck you, Knight. I don't want you. I want my money. All the money you stole from me. Every god-damn penny.*"

"Let her go and you'll get it."

The cackle I heard from the other man sent a shudder up my spine. It was identical to what I'd heard in the surveillance video.

When Judd lowered his chin and then raised it again, I peered around the corner.

Marshall Livingston held Mila around her waist and had a gun pressed firmly against her temple.

37

Adler

"*No! It can't be!*" I screeched when the woman played the video on her phone.

"Watch it," she seethed, shoving the screen into my face when I tried to look away. "Who is that, Adler? *Look at it and tell me!*"

"I'm going to be sick."

"I don't care if you throw up all over yourself; you're gonna watch every minute."

I shook my head as tears ran down my cheeks. There was no denying the man in the video was my father. It was the third time she made me watch and listen to the vile things he said and did.

"I didn't know. I swear I didn't know," I cried.

"Where's your father now, Adler?"

When I shook my head, she slammed her fist into my nose and then grabbed the hair on the back of my head. "*Where...is...he?*"

"He's in Texas," I cried as blood poured from my broken nose.

38

Mila

I breathed as deeply as I could through my nose and then let it out through my mouth, counting the seconds as I tried to slow my heartbeat. If today was the day I'd die, I wouldn't give Marshall Fucking Livingston the satisfaction of showing fear or begging for my life.

Listening to the two men argue, I got a clear picture of what had happened with Sybil. My father didn't kill Sybil; Marshall Livingston had when she refused to hand over the flash drive with the documents he'd paid her to steal from Knighthawk. Instead, my sister ran from the same house where we all were now. Marshall had gone after her, firing into the darkness, but lost her. Until Adler told him he was on his way to Texas with me, Marshall believed she'd gotten away.

He'd sneered when he told my father that, instead, his son told him that I was with the medical examiner, identifying my sister's body.

"You killed your own flesh and blood," my father yelled at him.

"How is that different than you abandoning yours?"

"Tell me this, Marshall," I heard my father say. "Did you rape my wife?"

The man holding the gun to my head laughed. At that moment, I wanted to kill him more than I ever had before. He didn't answer, but he didn't need to. His cackle gave both me and my father the answer.

I studied my father's face, watching the emotions play out on it. I saw both pain and fear, but then, I saw something else.

My father's eyes flashed as though he'd seen something, or someone, in the direction of the barn. Seconds later, I saw him slowly lower and then raise his head. It was a fraction of an inch, but I saw it. Was it a signal of some kind? Was someone else here? Was it Decker?

"What's it going to be Livingston? You kill her and you won't get a goddamn penny, and that's if you live long enough to see the inside of a prison cell. Let her go and we'll negotiate."

39

Decker

While I listened to Judd try to negotiate with Marshall, I sent a message to Rile, telling him that Mila was being held at gunpoint and that he should communicate with me through the headset.

"Understood," I heard Rile respond through my earpiece.

"Where are the records being stored?" I heard Marshall yell at Judd.

"In a safe location."

"Tell me where, you goddamn mother fucker!"

I peered around the corner and saw Livingston tighten his grip on Mila.

I was running out of time. There was no clear path for resolution here. Even if Judd told him where the files were, Marshall wouldn't let either of them just walk away. If only I had a way to tell Judd to give Marshall something, even if it was a lie. At least then the man would attempt some kind of move. While there was a fifty-fifty chance Livingston would shoot Mila first, my gut told me the man would shoot Judd.

"We have eyes on the scene," I heard Rile say.

"I have a clean shot from the south," Edge added.

I was on the north side of the house, and the gun Marshall held on Mila was in his right hand. If I fired, there was a chance Livingston might jerk, causing his gun to go off.

"Take it," I responded at the exact same moment Livingston lowered his arm and fired at Judd. Edge's shot went off a split-second later, hitting Marshall in the head. I surged forward as both men fell to the ground and caught Mila in my arms.

"You're safe. Everything is okay," I muttered, repeating myself as I walked her away from the scene.

Her skin was cold and clammy, breathing shallow, and her heart rate had to be skyrocketing based on what I could feel when I rested my fingers on her pulse. When I felt her legs give out, I caught her a second time and held her in my arms.

"Shh," I whispered. "Everything is okay. You're safe." I carried her over to the Bummer, set her in the front seat, and then raced around to the driver's side.

As I drove back to the ranch, I glanced over at Mila every few seconds. Her back was ramrod straight as she stared out the front window.

I pulled up to my garage and opened the door, but didn't drive inside. I parked and came around to open her door. When I took her hand, Mila turned her head and looked at me. "Is he dead?" she asked.

"Livingston is, sweetheart."

"What about my dad?"

"I don't know."

Mila slowly got out of the Bummer and held tight to me as I walked her inside. Once I had the door from the garage to the house open, I picked her up and carried her the rest of the way. I didn't stop until I got to my bedroom, where I laid her on my bed. I brushed the hair from her face and looked into her eyes. "I'll be right back, okay?"

"Okay," she whispered, nodding.

I rushed to the front of the house, went out and locked up the Bummer, came inside, and closed the garage door. On my way back to the bedroom, I sent a message to Rile.

Judd's condition?

Critical. Transporting now, came the quick reply.

I went into my room and toed off my boots. I sat on the edge of the bed and slid Mila's shoes off before lying down next to her.

She rolled to her side and lifted her head so I could put my arm around her before resting her head on my chest.

"I took my phone out to call you. He came up behind me."

I nodded, unsure where she was going with this, but knowing she needed to talk.

"I was going to tell you how sorry I was for the way I acted."

"You don't need to apologize for anything, Mila."

"I don't know why I got so upset with you. It wasn't fair. You didn't do anything but tell me what you discovered."

"It doesn't matter. You're here and you're safe. That's all I care about."

"Marshall killed Sybil, not my father."

"Did he confess?"

"He taunted my dad with it, but I don't think he cared."

"I'm sure somewhere deep inside he cared, Mila."

"He asked Marshall if he raped my mother."

"Did he confess to that too?"

"Not with words."

"Why was your father there?"

"I don't know, really. I called him earlier and told him I wanted money. He asked where I was. Maybe he came to give it to me; maybe he came to tell me he never would." Mila rested her chin on my chest and looked into my eyes. "How did you know to come?"

"I left shortly after you and Grinder did. I needed some time alone. When I came back, Grinder said he'd left you at the house alone."

She turned her head so her cheek rested on my heart.

"I sent a text to Rile. He said your father's condition is critical and he's being transported to the ER now."

"Okay," she whispered.

Mila was quiet for so long that I thought she may have fallen to sleep, but when I angled my head to check, her eyes were glassy and fixated on nothing.

"What are you thinking about, sweetheart?"

"Adler."

"What about him?"

"So many things. His father is dead. Someone should tell him." She sighed. "I wonder if he knew Marshall killed my sister and that she was his sister too." She paused. "What about his mother?"

"I don't know much about her." In everything I'd learned about Marshall Livingston, I found very little about his wife.

"Will he be arrested?"

"Adler?"

She nodded.

"I don't know the answer to that question either. It will depend on what all he knew, what his involvement was."

"Do you think he knew all along that his father attacked me?"

I could say without any hesitation at all that I hated Adler Livingston, but that didn't mean I believed the man knew the extent of his father's anger. Maybe madness would be a better word.

"I don't think so," I finally said. "He may have been his father's pawn, but my gut tells me he wouldn't have hurt you."

"Thank you for saying that, Decker."

My phone vibrated in my pocket. I closed my eyes and took a deep breath. As much as I wanted to ignore whoever and whatever it was, I knew I couldn't. I pulled it out and swiped the screen with my thumb.

Judd Knight didn't make it. The text was from Grinder, not Rile or Edge, so it didn't surprise me when the next text that came over said, *Please give my condolences to Mila.*

I dropped the phone on the bed and wrapped my other arm around Mila, holding her as tight as I could without hurting her.

"He's gone, isn't he?"

"Yes, Mila, he is."

"Now I'm really alone."

I knew from her staggered breathing and the dampness I felt on my shirt that Mila was crying.

I could tell her she wasn't alone; that she had me, but I knew that wouldn't be enough or what she needed. I'd been in her life a handful of days, and no matter how many times I reassured her that she could depend on me, count on me, be with me, none of that would change the fact that Mila now saw herself as an orphan. Whether I'd been in her life the last few years or not, didn't change the fact that Judd Knight had just abandoned his daughter for the second time—and this go-around, it was permanent.

40

Mila

Decker stood by my side through everything. He took me to the cabin on Bluebell Creek and went with me to the funeral home and cemetery to make arrangements for Sybil's services.

He held my hand when my father's attorney told me that in absence of any other heir, I'd inherited all of my father's holdings, and was now a very wealthy woman.

He stood in the back of the room when I met with Knighthawk's board of directors and told them I wanted nothing to do with my father's business.

When I told Deck I couldn't handle making arrangements for my father's services, he said he'd handle it, and that was the last I heard of it.

He sat next to me when the woman they all called Casper came to the house to tell me that while Adler Livingston was a piece of dog crap of a human being, she didn't believe he knew anything about his father's nefarious activities. Casper also told me that Adler'd moved out of my apartment building and that it was up for sale.

Every day, Decker helped me clean up the old house that now belonged to me, as well as make arrangements to turn my grandfather's house over to the bank.

In the three weeks since my father died, Decker had slept by my side every night without doing anything more than kiss my forehead before I fell asleep.

He never once asked whether I planned to stay in Texas or return to Boston. He didn't ask what I planned to do with the money and everything else I'd inherited from my father. He didn't ask anything of me.

As I walked through my life in a daze, he held my hand and guided me. Now, as we sat out on the steps of the front porch, I needed to give him the answers to all the questions he didn't ask.

"I'm going back to Boston," I began.

"Okay," Decker answered without looking at me.

"I made a life for myself there."

He nodded but didn't speak.

"I want you to know how much I appreciate everything you've done for me."

He turned his head then, and looked into my eyes. "I would do anything for you, Mila."

"Texas isn't my home, Decker. It hasn't been for a very long time. Even when I used to live here, it wasn't."

He turned his head and looked around, maybe as if he wanted to tell me that I did belong here, but he didn't.

"I'm leaving tomorrow," I said, standing to go inside. I heard the screen close behind me and knew Decker hadn't followed.

I slept at the house alone for the first time that night, but before Decker left, he told me he'd be by in the morning to take me to the airport.

"My flight leaves at ten," I'd told him, somehow knowing he wouldn't ask.

41

Decker

When I got back from dropping Mila off and went into the barn, Quint was there, waiting for me.

"Well?"

"Well what? She's gone."

Quint lowered his head and shook it. He and his wife, Darrow, had gotten back from their honeymoon yesterday morning, and last night, I had told him about everything that happened while they were gone, including the part about how I'd fallen in love with Mila Knight.

"Did you tell her?"

I shook my head. "No use."

"Seriously, Deck? Have you learned nothing from me?"

While Quint did have a point, given he'd almost lost Darrow because he was too stubborn to tell her how he felt, that didn't mean my situation with Mila was the same.

"Her life is in Boston. Mine is here."

"Darrow's life is in London. Mine is here."

"But it doesn't have to be. You've got me here, running the place. I could never leave you in charge."

Quint laughed and flipped me off. "You know those things you see that at the end of a person's life, they won't remember the hours they worked or the cars they bought, but they'll remember the time they spent with people they love?"

"What...the fuck...are you talking about?"

"You know...like those priceless commercials. Ice skates, fifty bucks. Ice skating with your kids, priceless."

"You've lost it. The man I knew, who's been my best friend since high school, is gone. I don't know who the hell you are."

Quint laughed again. "It's love, man. It changes you. Pretty soon you'll be quoting this stuff back to me."

"No, Quint. I won't be." It felt good to laugh, even for a few minutes, but the reality was, things weren't going to work out between me and Mila like they had for Quint and Darrow.

"How did you leave things?"

"I left her at the airport." I knew that wasn't my friend meant, but I was done talking about it. "I'm gonna ride out."

"I'll go with you."

42

Mila

Home, I thought, looking out the plane's window as we made our descent into Logan. I couldn't wait to stop at my favorite market and pick up some fresh seafood, go home, and relax in the oasis I'd created for myself in my four-hundred-square-foot apartment.

It might take me some time to get used to the fact that I could sit in front of my air conditioner in my bra and panties if I wanted to without worrying that someone was about to invade my privacy.

Tomorrow, after I unpacked and did some laundry, I'd look for a new job. It didn't matter that I didn't need the money; my life had never been about money.

If there was ever a perfect illustration of money not buying happiness, it would be my father's life. In the end, it was his money that was his downfall.

As I walked through security and out of the terminal, I looked at the people holding signs with the names of those they were picking up. It wasn't the first time since I left Texas that I felt the stabbing pain of missing Decker. That began as soon as he drove away after dropping me off at the curbside check-in. Even though it made no sense for him to do so, and I had no right to expect it, part of me thought he'd park and walk me in. When I leaned over to kiss him goodbye, he turned just slightly and kissed my cheek.

Looking out the window as the driver of the car service I'd called from the airport pulled up in front of my building, I didn't feel the same giddy anticipation as when I'd gazed at the city from the plane. And when I got out of the car, the driver popped the trunk but didn't get out to help me with my bag. That never would've flown in Texas.

I walked down the three steps that led from the sidewalk to the building's entrance. Had it always been this dirty and grungy? I fiddled with the key that I'd forgotten always stuck, and when I stopped to get my mail, there was a card in it saying I had to pick it up from the post office since it had been full to over-flowing.

Instead of climbing the stairs, I took the elevator. By the second floor, I remembered why I rarely did in the past. It smelled. Horribly, in fact.

These were all things I knew, even if they hadn't been at the forefront of my memory. That was why I'd painstakingly decorated my apartment in a way that would transport me from the griminess of the city.

I unlocked the door and stood on the threshold, waiting for that feeling of peace to envelop me. It didn't. My decor didn't look cool; it looked old, and not in a good way like that of the house off Old Austin Highway.

Leaving my bag next to the closet door, I went into the kitchen and saw my geraniums were dead, and looking out at my tiny patio, I saw the bougainvillea was dead too. It was to be expected; I'd been gone over a month, but still, looking at the sorry state of the place I'd consider my oasis, left me feeling depressed.

The next day, when I picked up my mail, there was another letter from Northeastern College of Music in the pile, this time saying they'd changed their mind and were renewing my contract, after all.

Instead of feeling elated, it pissed me off. First of all, the semester was about to begin and I was completely unprepared. Second, why did they put me through all the worry if they were going to change their mind?

I dropped the rest of the mail on the table inside the door to my apartment and then walked the two blocks to Northeastern's faculty administration building.

"Miss Knight, it's so good to see you," proclaimed the receptionist who'd barely looked up from her desk the last time I was there and certainly hadn't known my name.

"Um…yeah…hi. I received this letter and—"

"Mila, welcome back," said Dr. Statler, head of my department, as he came out of the provost's office. "Great timing. Come in. Dr. Berry would love to get the chance to talk with you since you're here."

What the fuck was going on? Before I'd gotten the letter saying they weren't renewing my contract, I'd been an adjunct instructor, aka lowest on the totem pole. Why then, did the provost want to talk to me?

"Come in," repeated the provost, who I'd never met before.

"Dr. Berry, may I present Mila Knight. She is the associate professor candidate I mentioned—also an NMC alum."

"Yes, yes," said the man, stepping forward to shake my hand. "It's a pleasure to meet you. May I call you Mila?"

"Of course," I said, looking between Dr. Berry and Dr. Statler. Associate professor? Where had that come from? "Wait a minute," I mumbled.

Both men stopped talking midsentence. I pulled the letter out of my handbag and looked at the date. Coincidentally, it was sent two weeks after my father's death, and one day after the *Wall Street Journal* article reported his passing along with the news that I was the sole heir to his fortune.

"I stopped in today to let you know that I cannot accept your offer of a contract renewal—"

"You do understand that our intention is to bring you back as an associate professor rather than an adjunct instructor?" said Dr. Statler.

"I do, and thank you, but I am relocating and will no longer be living in Boston."

"How disappointing to hear," said Dr. Berry, eyeing Dr. Statler.

"Where will you be relocating?" asked the red-in-the-face head of my former department.

"Texas. As I'm sure you're aware, I have recently inherited my father's business holdings." I turned around to leave, but looked over my shoulder. "Have a nice afternoon, gentlemen."

I stalked out of the office and back out to the street. I kept walking without any idea of where I was going, but eventually, I ended up at the same park where Adler and I had been the night I got the call about Sybil's murder. Of course I hadn't known it was a murder then. I also hadn't known that Adler Livingston was the worst kind of man...other than his rapist father. The other thing I hadn't known was that Sybil was only my half-sister. Not that it made any difference. My only regret about Sybil was that we'd never managed to become closer. If

I had the chance to do everything over again, I'd be a better role model to my younger sibling.

The bench where I'd gone to return my sister's call that night was empty. I walked over and ran my hand over the back of it. So much life had happened since that night. So much death too.

Instead of sitting there, I walked over to the area in front of the park's bandshell and sat in the grass. As Casper said, Adler was a piece of crap of a human being, but that didn't stop me from missing him some-times. That didn't mean I ever wanted to talk to him or see him again, but he had been my friend for four years, and in that time, we'd had fun.

My first night back in Boston, I thought about call-ing some of the friends I'd made both when I was a student and an instructor at the college, but when I ran down the mental list of who, there wasn't anyone I felt like talking to.

I didn't today either. At least no one in Boston. The person I really wanted to talk to was back in Texas, and I'd just lied to my former boss, saying that's where I planned to relocate.

But had it been a lie? What was there for me here? Even if things didn't go anywhere between me and

Decker, there was still more for me in my home state than there had ever been for me here.

My fingers ached to play the piano, and while I could now afford to buy one, it meant I'd have to move in order to have enough space. Was there anywhere else in Boston I'd want to live? Nowhere was coming to mind.

In Texas, I already had a home.

43

Decker

"Mind if I ride out with you?" Edge asked when he came into the barn and found me in the office.

"You ask me that every day."

"You aren't the easiest asshole to get along with these days," shouted Quint from his perch on the gate of an empty stall.

I didn't bother to raise my head when I flipped my friend off.

Edge tossed an envelope on the corner of my desk.

"What's that?"

"Property report on the Brandywine Ranch."

"Brandywine? Why?"

Edge turned around and made eye contact with Quint. Both men turned and looked at me.

"*Jesus*. What?"

"He doesn't know," said Quint, coming in to sit on the edge of the desk.

I stood up, ready to walk out, but Quint rested a hand on my shoulder. "Mila's farmhouse is on the outer edge. She probably has no idea what she's got there. Gotta be at least a thousand acres."

"*Shit,*" I said, shrugging Quint's hand away and walking over to Ike's stall. I saddled him up as fast as I could, threw a leg over, and edged the horse out into the wide open.

There was absolutely no chance that I could tell Mila how I felt about her now. She'd think I was after the same thing every person she came in contact with probably was. She'd think I'd want a piece of her pie when all I wanted was her. No ranch, not even a farmhouse. Just Mila. Whatever she wanted, I'd give her. Wherever she wanted to go, I wanted to be by her side, holding her hand.

The stupidest thing I'd ever done was not get on that plane with her and never look back. In the short time since she'd been gone, I realized that the King-Alexander Ranch meant something to me because it was home. The people I loved and cared for had always been there. Even after Z left, it was still his home, the place he always came back to no matter where in the world his job took him.

Why hadn't I realized that sooner? Why couldn't I see that home was where my heart was—and now my heart was with Mila.

I rode past the Schoolhouse pasture, coaxed Ike into jumping the fence, and kept going. Mila was gone, but I still needed to feel close to her.

As I got nearer to the house, I could swear I heard piano music. Maybe I'd spent so much time listening to Mila play, I heard it in my memory.

When I got close to the front door, I knew that what I heard wasn't inside my head. I tied Ike off and walked to the front door. I probably should've knocked, but I couldn't wait. I had to know who was in that house.

As I came around the corner, the first thing I saw was Mila's beautiful blonde hair cascading down her back in soft waves. I leaned against the open door frame, loving the way her body moved with the music. Loving the way she carried the most exquisite sounds I'd ever heard from her fingertips and into my ears. Loving her.

When I closed my eyes, I heard something I never had before. Mila was singing.

> *I'm so tired, but I can't sleep*
> *Standin' on the edge of something much too deep*
> *It's funny how we feel so much but cannot say a word*
> *We are screaming inside, but we can't be heard*
> *I will remember you. Will you remember me?*
> *Don't let your life pass you by*
> *Weep not for the memories*
> *I'm so afraid to love you*
> *But more afraid to lose...you.*

With the last word she sang, Mila turned around and held her hand out to me.

"What are you doing here?" I asked as I walked over to her.

"I remembered you and you remembered me, Decker. Don't you think that means something?" She stood and put her arms around me.

"I think it means everything."

"I love you, Decker."

"I love you, Mila. Just you."

"I know."

"Do you?" I asked.

She nodded.

"I need to say this, though."

"Go ahead."

"I don't care about a red cent you inherited or an acre of land or whatever else Judd Knight left you. If you told me you gave it all away, I wouldn't care. Not at all."

"There isn't anyone else on this earth I would believe if they said those words. Only you."

"You haven't answered my question. What are you doing here?"

"I hate Boston, but more importantly, I love you. I didn't belong there, Decker."

I smiled, tilted my head back, and looked up at the ceiling.

"What?" she asked, resting her hand on my heart.

"I rode out today knowing, or believing, it would be my last time."

"What do you mean?"

"I've made a lot of mistakes in my life, but the biggest one was not getting on that plane and going to Boston with you."

"You know where I want you to go with me now?"

I shook my head.

"Upstairs. Decker."

She took her phone out of her pocket and turned it off, so I did the same.

"Where's the other one?"

"Back at the ranch."

"Good. I don't want anyone or anything to interrupt us. I want you to show me what love is, Decker. Not just today..."

"Every day—for the rest of our lives, Mila.

Would you like a bonus chapter of DECKED?
Sign up to receive my newsletter by visiting:
https://www.subscribepage.com/heathersladeenews
Then shoot me an email, and
I'll send you the chapter!

———————————

Keep reading for a sneak peek

at the second book

in The Invincibles Series—

EDGED!

1

Edge

I had three more nights in Texas, and then I had to fly to Boston—a place I had zero interest in going, for a reason I didn't give a shit about.

If it were for work, that would be different. If there was a mission to be had, I was the first to raise my hand, more so now that I'd left the rules and regulations of MI5 behind and was a partner in the Invincible Intelligence and Security Group.

A partner's wife had first called us the Invincibles, and it took. Yeah, it sounded cocky as shit, but we all were, so what the hell?

I'd tried to get my best friend, Miles "Grinder" Stone, to come out with me tonight, but he was in what I referred to as his dark place.

The man had PTSD from a deployment with ISAF— the International Security Assistance Force—a NATO-led security mission in Afghanistan. I admired the guy enough to respect the times when he wasn't interested in socializing.

I could've invited Cortez "Rile" DeLéon, the eldest of the four partners, but that would be almost as bad as going out with my secondary school headmaster.

It wasn't as though I wouldn't know anyone at the Long Branch tonight or any other night. Most of the hands who worked on the King-Alexander Ranch, where I lived, frequented the place.

I pulled into the parking lot, surprised at how few cars were in it, and found a spot not too far from the entrance.

Climbing out of the 1957 Ford ranch pickup I'd borrowed, I slammed the creaky door closed. The locks had a tendency to stick, so I didn't bother trying to secure it. If any wanker tried to make off with it, this truck, like the rest of those at the ranch, was equipped with a tracking device that would allow the engine to be shut off remotely.

I hadn't done it yet, but if I was ever given the chance to, I'd press the kill button as soon as the driver hit a decent speed. For the Ford, that would be about seventy since the old thing wouldn't go much faster. I chuckled, thinking about the look on the bastard's face when the truck flipped end to end on one of the area's dirt roads.

It was hotter than Hades tonight with close to one hundred percent humidity, but I still wore my pearl snap shirt and pressed Cinch jeans. Anything else would get me tossed out of the Branch—as we affectionately called it—on my arse.

Walking past a newer edition pickup, I averted my eyes when I saw the front bench seat was occupied by a couple shagging. I was almost to the back bumper when I realized the sounds the woman was making weren't those of pleasure.

I spun around, wrenched open the door, grabbed the asshole by the shirt collar, and pulled him away from the woman I now could tell was trying to fight the guy off.

"What the fuck?" the guy slurred.

I threw him up against the truck next to his, and as I did, I got a whiff of alcohol.

Holding the drunk by the neck, I turned around to tell the woman to get dressed and get the hell out of there, but she was ahead of me. Instead of getting out of the passenger side, she climbed out the driver's side, walked straight over to the wanker, and slammed her knee into his crotch. I cringed thinking about how much that had to hurt.

When she threw a punch into the guy's gut, I thought I may have fallen in love at first sight.

I heard a car pull up and looked over my shoulder, surprised to see the sheriff. "Hey, Mac. Good timing."

"What's goin' on here?"

"The fucker tried to rape me," said the woman, wiping what looked like blood from a cut on her face.

I still had the guy by the back of the collar. I let him go, and he fell to the ground, hands on his crotch.

"I got this, Edge. You go on and get outta here."

"Thanks, mate. I owe you one." In my line of work, the last thing I could afford was to be a witness in a rape trial.

I walked over to the old Ford and was about to climb in when I heard a soft voice ask me to wait. When I turned around, the feisty woman who slammed her would-be rapist in the balls with her knee, got on her tiptoes and planted a kiss right on my lips. It wasn't a chaste one either. "Thanks, Edge," she said as she walked away.

I shook my head and climbed into the truck, wishing I could stay, but knowing I couldn't.

Two nights later, wanting to grab a pint before I left town for God knew how long, I went back to the Branch. It was harder to find a place to park tonight; it looked like the place was packed.

I pulled open the heavy door and made my way through the crowd. When I got up to the bar, the owner brought me a beer before I had a chance to order.

"This one's on her." He pointed to the end of the bar.

I looked to where he motioned and met the woman's eyes. "What's her name?"

"That's Rebel."

About the Author

I write stories set in places I love with characters I'd be happy to call friends. The women in my books are self-confident, successful, and strong, with wills of their own, and hearts as big as the Colorado sky. And the men are sublimely sexy, seductive alphas who rise to the challenge of capturing the sweet soul of a woman whose heart they'll hold in the palm of their hand forever.

I'm an Amazon best-selling author, and a PAN member of Romance Writers of America. I speak, teach, blog, am an executive sommelier, and all-around entrepreneur.

I grew up an East Coast girl, and then spent half my life on the West Coast. Now my husband, our two boys, and I happily call Colorado home.

I would love to hear from my readers, you can contact me at: heather@heatherslade.com

To keep up with my latest news and releases, please visit my website at: www.heatherslade.com to sign up for my newsletter.

MORE FROM HEATHER SLADE

Made in the USA
Monee, IL
10 March 2020